This man was cowboy to the hardened core.

He offered a brief smile. He had very even white teeth. "Heard Seamus sold this ol' place to a lawyer outta Cheyenne." He resettled his hat another centimeter or two up his forehead. "Guessing she's you."

She pushed her sunglasses into place again. "I'm not a lawyer." *Anymore.* "But I am the one who bought this place and the dog grooming business it came with." Sight unseen, so she guessed she got what she deserved, too.

He drew closer, not stopping until he stood right beside her in front of the door. She took a step sideways, reestablishing her personal space as he leaned down to study the key broken off inside the lock.

Then he straightened again and turned to her.

"Could be worse. It was supposed to rain today."

She looked at her twin reflections in his dark glasses, trying to decide whether or not there was a hint of humor in his deep voice. There was something about him that made her feel edgy.

Not in a fearful way.

In a "he's a man, you're a woman" sort of way.

Dear Reader,

What a year it has been. Not just for those of us writing and reading books, but for those inside the pages, as well.

This is true for Ros Pastore. She's struggling with the fallout of learning her father wasn't the man she believed him to be. She's a woman who has prided herself on never faltering; but faltering is all she feels like she is doing. So she turns her back on the past year and makes as big a life-altering change as she thinks she can. She goes from being a fearsome attorney to buying a dog grooming business. She likes dogs. How hard could it be?

Enter Trace Powell, the rancher neighbor who has his own past he's overcome.

The last thing she wants to do is make another mistake, but thanks to Trace's magic touch, Ros learns that love is the most life-altering thing of all.

Allison

A Rancher's Touch

ALLISON LEIGH

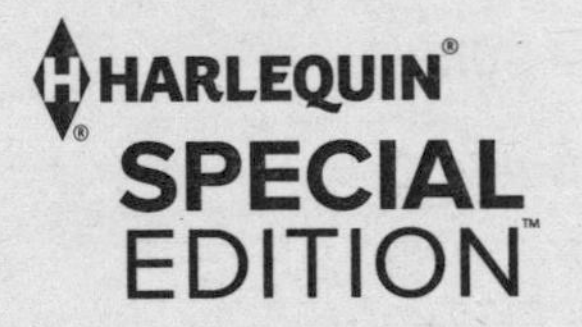

ISBN-13: 978-1-335-40809-9

A Rancher's Touch

This edition published by arrangement with Harlequin Books S.A.

For questions and comments about the quality of this book, please contact us at CustomerService@Harlequin.com.

Harlequin Enterprises ULC
22 Adelaide St. West, 40th Floor
Toronto, Ontario M5H 4E3, Canada
www.Harlequin.com

Printed in U.S.A.

Though her name is frequently on bestseller lists, **Allison Leigh**'s high point as a writer is hearing from readers that they laughed, cried or lost sleep while reading her books. She credits her family with great patience for the time she's parked at her computer, and for blessing her with the kind of love she wants her readers to share with the characters living in the pages of her books. Contact her at allisonleigh.com.

Books by Allison Leigh

Harlequin Special Edition

Return to the Double C

A Weaver Christmas Gift
One Night in Weaver...
The BFF Bride
A Child Under His Tree
Yuletide Baby Bargain
Show Me a Hero
The Rancher's Christmas Promise
A Promise to Keep
Lawfully Unwed
Something About the Season
The Horse Trainer's Secret
A Rancher's Touch

The Fortunes of Texas: Rambling Rose

The Texan's Baby Bombshell

The Fortunes of Texas: The Hotel Fortune

Cowboy in Disguise

Visit the Author Profile page
at Harlequin.com for more titles.

For my editor, Charles Griemsman,
with extra eyeglasses, extra patience
and extra good humor.
It is always a pleasure.

Chapter One

You get what you pay for.

Ros Pastore stared at the small building situated at the end of the one-lane road.

It was a single story with one part of the roof pitched and the other flat, and a brick chimney sticking up from the back like a stubby thumb. The siding was an indeterminate shade of *blech*, the original color long since faded away.

The front window took up most of the facade but the glass pane was covered by dozens of flyers, none of which looked remotely recent. Above the scarred wood door next to the window was a giant, hand-painted sign, not charming, or homespun, in any sort of way.

Poocheez.

The only moderately attractive element about the place was the tree growing in front of it, but even that wasn't perfect because its roots had caused the walkway leading to the front door to buckle and crack.

Her head swam and she swayed slightly.

Was it horror over the reality of her actions? Or was it simply that she hadn't eaten since breakfast the day before when she'd packed up everything she still owned and left Cheyenne once and for all?

You get what you pay for.

How many times had her father drilled those words into her head?

A hundred?

A million?

Ironically, her father, Martin Pastore, was now getting what he'd paid for, too. A sentence of seven years in the state penitentiary for multiple counts of fraud.

It could have been worse. Thanks to his lifelong legal career and the favors he'd racked up, he'd managed to avoid prosecution at the federal level in his plea deal. He'd still lost everything he'd built over the last thirty-five years. Money. Reputation. The law practice he'd founded that she'd made the center of her life since even before she'd gone to law school.

The truth was that it *should* have been worse.

Maybe that was to be her penance. Knowing that her father had gotten off too lightly for the crimes he'd committed.

Right under her nose.

She closed her eyes against the sight of the ugly little building. But that just left her to the mercy of the thoughts that had been squatting inside her head for the better part of the past year.

The real truth?

She deserved to lose everything she'd worked for just as much as her father deserved his prison sentence.

The jagged teeth of the key she'd picked up from the real estate office in Weaver dug into her fingers.

She exhaled, opened her eyes wide and faced the building.

Faced the future.

She'd bought it outright with the last bit of savings she had left. Not just this building located at the end of No Name Road. But the business it housed.

Rosalind Pastore, no-longer attorney-at-law. Dog-grooming business owner instead.

She'd *wanted* different. *Needed* different.

So she'd chosen different.

A different career. And particularly a different place, away from Cheyenne where conversations ground to a halt whenever she entered the room.

"Can't get much more different than this place," she muttered to herself.

She looked back up the narrow road. It was 2.2 miles to the highway. Once there, if she turned one way, it was about fifteen miles to Weaver. If she turned the other way, it was about the same distance to Braden.

Her mother lived in Braden.

Probably why she'd chosen to work with a real estate agent in Weaver.

One more thing for her to feel guilty about. She'd moved closer to Braden.

But not *that* close.

She pinched her eyes, annoyed with herself.

She felt herself sinking in the pity pool again.

But the whole reason she was here was to keep from drowning in it.

She yanked the smallest of her suitcases out of her trunk and carried it toward the grimy-looking door. Up close, it looked even worse. Even the doorknob looked covered in filth.

But if she got rid of the multitude of faded flyers in the window, scrubbed everything up and maybe painted some fresh wood stain on the door, it would surely look more inviting. That could be one of the first things she focused on.

A welcoming entrance.

She could almost hear the laughter of her former associates.

Ros Pastore. Worried about being welcoming.

Annoyance burbled at the edges of her nerves and she shoved the key into the lock and turned.

The key snapped off. Right in half.

She stared for a moment at the stub left attached to her key ring, then bent over to look at the half left inserted in the lock. It didn't budge when she tried to catch an edge of it with her fingernail.

She straightened, swearing under her breath, and let her suitcase drop to the ground. The expensive hard-side suitcase popped open, spewing the contents out onto the weeds sprouting through the cracked cement.

Her shoulders sank as she eyed the rainbow-hued mess. "Perfect. Just...freaking...perfect."

She kicked the side of the suitcase, which only

made her toes hurt and sent her zippered makeup bag toppling onto the sidewalk as well.

"Don't know about perfect," a deep voice drawled from behind her, "but I don't think kicking that thing is going to help the situation."

She whirled on her sandal and looked at the man standing near her Lexus.

She was too damn tired after the last year to be too startled by the sudden appearance of a guy in a cowboy hat leading a saddled horse down a country road.

Even if he did fit the description of tall, dark and deadly.

She lowered her chin and looked over the rims of her sunglasses at him. "Doesn't help, but I don't think it necessarily hurts, either." She sent a pointed look at the sign hanging above the door. "And it isn't as if I kicked a dog."

"Truc enough."

He was tall with shoulders wide as an ox. The parts of his face that weren't covered by sunglasses or the cowboy hat pulled low on his brow were covered by a dark beard. His green shirt was plain, his blue jeans were even plainer and his boots were as dusty as the cowboy hat on his head.

She'd been born and raised in Wyoming. Just because she'd had a privileged upbringing didn't mean she couldn't distinguish a man in a cowboy costume from a real cowboy.

This one looked cowboy to the hardened core.

"Speaking of." She eyed the big black horse standing docile alongside him. The animal's legs were spattered with mud. "Dog grooming's on the menu here. Not horse grooming."

The man looked over the rims of his sunglasses. "If you've ever shampooed a dirty dog, I'll eat my hat."

She'd spent two summers working at an animal shelter where she'd done nothing but shampoo and groom dirty dogs. Just because that had been more than twenty years ago didn't mean it didn't count.

"Hat looks a bit dusty to me, but then again it might add a little flavor when you start chewing."

He offered a brief smile. "Heard ol' Seamus sold this place sight unseen to a lawyer outta Cheyenne." He resettled his hat another centimeter or two up his forehead and pulled his sunglasses off altogether. His eyes were dark. "Guessing she's you."

She pushed her sunglasses into place again. "I'm not a lawyer." Not anymore.

He walked closer. "You're *not* the one who bought Poocheez?"

She looked up at the ugly sign again and tried not to sigh too loudly. "Yeah, I am the one—" heaven help her "—who did that. I'm just not a lawyer."

She heard the scrape of the man's boots and from the corner of her eye saw him draw closer. He didn't try to prevent his horse from straying to the thick grass tufting up from the narrow creek on the other side of the road.

The man didn't stop until he was standing right beside her in front of the door. "So what's the problem here?"

She was five-seven in her flat sandals. Her head barely reached his shoulder.

This was why she'd always worn heels. To give her more of an advantage. Even though she knew it was only a psychological one.

He smelled earthy. Like sagebrush and leather and summer sun.

Not unpleasant. But very, *very* masculine.

She took a step sideways, re-creating the personal space he'd just invaded. "Key broke in the lock." She jiggled the knob. It neither turned nor magically spit out the broken key.

"That the only key they gave you? There's a door 'round back, too."

It was a reasonable question. It just happened to rub her overworked nerves wrong. "If they'd given me two keys do you think I'd be standing here having a discussion about it with you?"

His dark gaze slid over her again. "Folks around these parts know how to depend on others, honey."

I depend on myself.

At least she didn't say it aloud. Her nerves were nearly shot, but she hadn't lost all sense.

She crossed her arms and watched him lean down to study the lock. He tried to catch a corner of the sheared-off key to work it free the way she had. Only he used a folding knife he'd pulled from his front pocket.

It wasn't any more effective than her fingernail method.

Then he straightened and thumbed his hat back another inch. The fine ray of lines spreading from his eyes were an indicator that, hat or no, he spent a lot of time squinting in the sun. "Hope you're not one of those people who're prone to thinking everything's a sign."

She jiggled the knob again, even though she knew it would do no good. It was that or kick the door, which would be equally fruitless. "Right now, I'm beginning to wonder if that's where I've been going wrong."

"Could be worse." He slid his sunglasses back in place. "It was supposed to rain today."

She looked at her twin reflections in his dark glasses. She tried to figure out whether or not there was a hint of humor in his deep voice. And why she was even curious.

She'd never been attracted to bearded hulks. Particularly ones who tossed around words like *honey* to complete strangers.

But he definitely made her edgy.

In that "he's a man, you're a woman" sort of way.

It was annoying, if for no other reason than that the past year had done nothing but prove how miserable she was with relationships. Personal. Professional.

You name it and she'd failed at it.

In spectacular fashion.

"I'm Ros," she said abruptly. "Ros Pastore. New owner of Poocheez whether I can get through the door or not. Is there something I can do for you?"

He stuck out his hand. "Trace Powell. And it might be more like what I can do for you."

She clasped his hand. Briefly.

Long enough to note the warmth. The calluses. The lack of rings. And the fact that her hand felt small and delicate inside of his.

Delicate was supposed to be something her father had groomed out of her early on. In its place, he'd cultivated competitiveness. Drive.

And look where it had gotten her.

She pulled her hand away and splayed her fingers on her hip, pretending she didn't have a pile of panties from the suitcase scattered at her feet. "I might as well apologize in advance if your name is supposed to mean something to me, Trace Powell."

He pointed over her shoulder toward the land beyond the thicket of trees growing at the end of the road. "I'm your nearest neighbor."

That she hadn't expected.

Which was probably stupid of her.

The man hadn't driven up with a dog that needed a shampoo. He'd shown up on horseback.

But when the real estate agent had described the rancher next door, she'd expected something different. Though now, she was hard-pressed to figure out why.

"You own the Bar-H Ranch?"

He lifted a finger to the brim of his cowboy hat. "Yes, ma'am. And *I* might as well apologize in advance for saying that you paid Seamus too much for this heap of lumber."

"You know how much I paid, too?"

"Doesn't matter the amount. Seamus got the better end of the deal. Maybe you should've found some time in your schedule to see what you were getting into before you signed on the dotted line."

He was right, of course, but she didn't welcome him pointing it out to her. "Just what is it that you think you can do for me, Mr. Powell?" She heard a snicker somewhere in the libido corner of her brain.

"Trace." He smiled slightly. "I've got a spare key."

"Why, exactly, do you have a spare key to *my* property?" It wasn't going to be just her workplace, but where she would live.

The words of the online advertisement were permanently imprinted in her mind.

Dog-grooming storefront attached to private living accommodations. Business equipment and home furnishings included. Five acres conveniently located.

"It's been your property for a whopping twenty-four hours." Trace's voice deepened with irony. "And Seamus gave the key to me a long time ago. During better days." He made a point of stepping back a few paces and looking at the building. "I'm sure it's apparent to a smart woman like you that he isn't much for making changes. That definitely includes the locks."

If she were smart would she have bought Pooch-eez on a whim and one-too-many bottles of wine?

The only smart thing she'd done had been to make certain that Seamus Shaw was contractually obligated to see her through the transition of the business and help make sure that the part-time groomer—some guy name Drake—stayed on staff.

She'd given up practicing law, but she hadn't given up her brain.

Despite appearances to the contrary.

"Do you have the key with you?" She held out her palm even though she really didn't expect the man to produce it right that second.

"Won't take me long to get it." He whistled sharply and the horse lifted its head from the creek and obediently clip-clopped back across the road toward him. "Don't go anywhere."

Ros hid a grimace.

Where would she go?

She crouched down to scoop her underwear back into the suitcase while he met the horse halfway and swung up into the saddle, looking like he'd been doing it all his life.

She heard him cluck and the horse launched forward.

The only thing missing from the image of him riding off was a sunset.

She rubbed her face and looked back at the building.

Her building.

"It's you and me now, Poocheez." She jiggled the doorknob. "So this better *not* be a sign."

Chapter Two

"Didja see her?"

Trace looked at his son as he hunted in the junk drawer for the keys. "Who?" Though he knew perfectly well.

"The lady who bought Grandpa's business."

"Yeah." He shoved aside a paintbrush that had dried stiff. "I'm not sure you should expect too much where she's concerned, Drake. I doubt she'll stay long."

"Why not?"

Because Ros Pastore looked too glossy for that old hovel.

"She's from Cheyenne. She's used to a different sort of life." He swept aside the junk to search the other back corner of the drawer.

"How do you know that?"

Because I said so was one of those phrases Trace hated using as a parent.

I can just tell was also a cop-out.

"Most people born and raised in town tend to stay in town. And you know how much dog-grooming business she's likely to have. She'll be lucky if she makes enough to pay the water bill." Although, considering the fancy silver Lexus and designer luggage, money was probably not an issue for the lady lawyer who claimed she wasn't a lawyer.

Which begged the question as to why she was here in the first place.

Not that he was curious.

Or annoyed that Seamus had thwarted him again when it came to that little island of land. Now Seamus was off on some beachside resort in Mexico supposedly living out his lifelong dream.

He hoped Ros Pastore cut her losses and unloaded the property again as soon as possible. Trace would be first in line to pick it up. Seamus no longer owned it, so his former father-in-law couldn't very well stop him this time.

He pulled the drawer clean out and upended the contents on the oak kitchen table.

Drake abandoned the jar of peanut butter he'd been mining with a spoon. "Grandpa had enough business to keep us busy." He sucked at the spoon as he watched Trace scatter the odds and ends in his hunt for the elusive key. "Whatcha looking for?"

"Grandpa's key to Poocheez."

Drake got up and walked into the mudroom. He returned a few seconds later with the old key chain dangling from a finger.

"Where was it?"

Drake pulled the spoon from his mouth. "On the hook."

Naturally. Where the damn thing was supposed to be.

But living with an eight-year-old son had taught Trace that, generally speaking, nothing ever was where it was supposed to be.

He took the key chain and pointed at the dishes piled in the sink. "It's your turn to load the dishwasher."

Drake made a face. It was July. Already one month into the three months of summer that Drake stayed with Trace full-time. During the school year, Drake only came out to the ranch every other weekend. The rest of the time he was in Braden with his mom.

Summertime, though, meant the reverse.

That time belonged to Trace.

He was smart enough now to cherish it.

"You load the dishwasher at your mom's, too," he reminded the boy.

"Don't like doin' it there, either." Drake shuffled on his bare feet over to the sink.

Trace hid a smile. "When I get back we can go over to Weaver. I've got some business to take care of in town and then we can have lunch there."

Drake's skinny shoulders rose a little. "At Ruby's?"

"If you want. And while you're at it, grab a shower."

"Dad—"

"You smell like you've been swimming in the creek again." He headed for the door. "I won't be long."

He'd already washed down Festus and put him out in the pasture, but instead of taking the truck and driving over to Seamus's place, he went on foot. It would give his son more time to finish his chores.

It also gave Trace plenty of time before he had to see his new neighbor again.

He was forty years old. He'd been married and divorced. He'd been all over the world with the military. He had plenty of experience when it came to life. And women.

But it had been a while since he'd met someone who caused as much of a jolt as Ros Pastore did.

He wasn't really sure why.

She was beautiful. No doubt about that. Her hair had gleamed nearly black in the sunshine, reaching halfway down to her narrow waist. The eyes that had flashed at him over the rim of her dark sunglasses were strikingly blue. Even in skinny jeans and a plain white T-shirt, she'd looked like a million bucks.

But there were plenty of beautiful women in the world who didn't spark more than a speck of his interest.

Humor. Compassion. Those were the kinds of things that drew him to a woman these days.

Ros, on the other hand, seemed as brittle as the key that broke off in Seamus's lock.

He curled his fingers around the key chain, and lengthened his stride. Not because he was in any hurry to see her again.

But because summer—like everything else in life—didn't last forever.

She had vacated her perch by the front door when he reached it, and the pile of lacy underwear that she'd nonchalantly ignored earlier was gone as well.

He walked around to the back of the oddball building where the door to the living quarters was located.

She wasn't there, either, though the suitcases had been deposited neatly on the square of brick pavers that Trace himself had laid what felt like a lifetime ago.

He pushed the key into the lock. It grated as he turned it, but at least it all worked the way it was intended. He left the key there and pushed open the door enough to set the suitcases inside.

Sunshine flooded the kitchen, but Trace flicked the light switch just inside the doorway anyway. He wasn't surprised that he got no results. He knew that Seamus hadn't ever occupied the residence, he'd just used the grooming business up front, so it was a toss-up whether the lightbulb was merely burned out or if there was no electricity at all. The ancient gas stove gave no clue. Neither did the fridge. Except for the rodent curled in the nest sitting on the floor, everything in the room had the air of abandonment.

He left the door open. Fresh air could only help the odor situation going on in there.

He didn't figure she'd gone far since her car hadn't moved an inch. The property was hers whether he liked it or not. She'd find the key and it was no business of his if she was equipped to deal with the state of the place.

She'd settle in and take care of it, or she wouldn't.

He was betting on the latter.

And was honest enough with himself to admit that he was hoping for just that.

He turned on his heel and set off back in the direction he'd come. His ranch house wasn't visible from here because of the rocky terrain. A couple hundred yards out, though, and the roof of his barn would be.

He'd collect Drake. They'd drive into Weaver for his meeting with Squire Clay. Trace had finally convinced the old cattle baron to sell back the couple thousand acres he'd bought from Trace's mom a decade ago and they had some papers to sign.

Roast beef sandwiches and chocolate malts with Drake afterward at Ruby's café was a suitable celebration as far as Trace was concerned. They could even spend the rest of the afternoon fishing at the lake out on Rambling Mountain.

Just thinking of it made him smile.

Then he heard a muffled scream, cut off mid-screech.

He sighed, wishing he'd walked faster and been out of earshot.

But he turned around and jogged back to the house.

Because his sense of duty was too ingrained to ignore.

She was in the kitchen, her hand clamped against her mouth as she stared at the nest in front of the refrigerator. She looked over at him when he stepped through the doorway.

He pulled off his hat and held it at his side. Aside from the expression in her vivid blue eyes, she looked unharmed. “You okay?”

She nodded, though she didn’t lower her hand from her mouth. Instead, she pointed at the nest with the sunglasses she was holding.

Even though he could see it was empty now, he walked closer and looked down at the mess of leaves, fibers and Lord only knew what.

“It ran out the door.” Her words were muffled behind her hand. “Through…through my legs.” He could see her entire body shudder with revulsion. “All teeth and eyes and a horrid tail—”

“Possum,” he said. “More afraid of you than you were of it.”

She finally lowered her hand and raked her hair back from her face. “Not possible.” She shuddered again, dancing a little jig as if creepy-crawlies were climbing around inside her clothes. Then she suddenly stilled and shot him a narrow-eyed look. “How do *you* know it was a possum?”

Because he’d seen it when he’d moved her suitcases inside.

Sometimes discretion was the wiser course. Another lesson he’d mastered courtesy of the US Marine Corps.

"Educated guess," he lied. Then sopped his conscience with a little truth. It wasn't her fault Seamus wouldn't sell to him. "Seamus mentioned once that he had a problem with them."

She looked even more horrified. *"Them?"*

"Once you clean up this place and start occupying it, they'll probably find another location to nest." He tapped his hat against the side of his thigh. "Don't think kitchens are their natural habitat."

"Really?" She sounded sarcastic. "So happy to have a possum expert close at hand."

"Could be worse."

She raised an eyebrow. "How?"

"Thing could have had babies."

She finally lowered her hands from her hair, but only so she could shake them at her sides and execute another few steps of her shuddering jig of disgust.

He swallowed the urge to smile and looked away from her bare, finely boned ankles.

In her place, he'd have wanted to take a fire hose to the place just to wash it down. Outside and inside.

Maybe he'd even wait to apply said fire hose until after a judicious application of lit matches.

It was a thought worth keeping. For the future, of course.

Trace's interest in the property had nothing to do with the structure that Seamus had cobbled together all those years ago. It was in the land itself.

She was muttering something under her breath. Not directed at him but at herself.

He had good hearing.

"This is what I deserve," she was saying.

He squelched another sigh. "Seamus used to keep a shovel up front. I'll see if it's still there." He headed around her into the minuscule living area dominated by the ugliest sleeper couch this side of the landfill. He flipped the latch on the door that separated the living area from the grooming suite and walked through.

The shovel was where he expected—in the crowded storage room. He returned to the kitchen and scooped up the nest, carried it outside and dumped it into Seamus's blackened burn barrel. The barrel was already filled halfway with leaves.

Ros had followed him outside. She'd pushed her sunglasses up on top of her head, so that they were holding her hair back from her face. She was hugging her arms around herself as she watched him.

The clear sparkling stones dangling from her ears nearly to her shoulders possessed more color than her expertly made-up face. She was too magazine-perfect to look vulnerable.

But that didn't mean she wasn't.

"If it's any comfort, the grooming area isn't so bad." He left the shovel propped against the wall near the door. "Seamus never did use the living quarters 'cept to maybe store stuff."

"But he *did* use the grooming area?"

"Yeah." He didn't want to tell her how rarely. She'd find that out soon enough. Seamus had only been open for business on the weekends when Drake was around to help out. The fact that Seamus doted on Drake was one of his few saving graces as far as Trace was concerned. Seamus knew Drake loved dogs and if not for him begging otherwise, Trace was certain the old man would have closed up Poocheez long before now. "Lightbulb is burned out in the kitchen, but there are extras in the storage room. You'll see 'em easily enough." He jammed his hat on his head. If he wished her good luck settling in, he'd come off as sarcastic or unfeeling.

He'd been guilty of both plenty of times, but he felt a little bad for her.

"There are a few motels around. Nothing fancy, but respectable enough if you want to get this place more habitable before—"

She was already shaking her head.

She unfolded her arms and rubbed her palms down her hips. "This is the bed I've bought."

And he thought she might need a mental competency exam as a result. But he had to give her credit for sounding decisive.

"Do you have a cell phone?"

Her eyes narrowed slightly, though she reeled it off.

He pulled his phone out of his pocket and dialed it. He let it ring a few times on his side—he didn't hear hers ringing at all—and then ended the call. Now the number would still be available on her device. It was her decision if she wanted to keep it or not. "Call if you need to."

Her chin lifted slightly. "I appreciate the offer but I won't."

He looked away from the set curve of her rosy lips, only to land on her ankles again. He couldn't remember ever really noticing a woman's ankles. Legs. Butt. Breasts. He appreciated any and all, though he liked to think he factored the entire person into the equation of appeal. "Then call if you want."

"I don't want, either."

He smiled ruefully. "In that case, you're a stronger person than I am." He pointed at the burn barrel. "It's already getting too full. Don't add anything more in there before you burn."

Her eyebrows twitched together. "Burn?"

He pantomimed striking a match. "Light it up. Burn it to ash. Keep a hose handy just in case things get out of control." Then he flicked the brim of his hat and made himself turn to leave.

The beautiful new neighbor was just a passing intrigue. She'd leave sooner or later.

It was simply a matter of waiting her out.

Meanwhile, the summer days were flying by.

And he had a son's company to enjoy.

Chapter Three

"Rosalyn, please. You're welcome to stay with us. There's no need for you—"

"Mother." Ros's hand tightened around her cell phone. "I'm *fine*." She didn't let her eyes wander beyond the kitchen, which had taken her the entire day to clean. "I appreciate the offer." Guilt made her say the words that had felt so much easier when she'd used them earlier with Trace Powell.

It was quite the statement that she was more comfortably polite with a complete stranger than she was with her own flesh and blood.

Meredith Templeton's sigh was audible through the phone. "You know Carter and I have the room."

"I know." She tugged at the braid she'd twisted her hair into shortly after the rancher next door had left. She—queen of independence—had felt an unfamiliar urge to call out to him. To ask him not to leave her there.

"I need to get used to being here," she said aloud. The words were as much for herself as for her mother.

"Carter drove by there when Archer and Nell told us what you were planning," Meredith said. "To say he was appalled is putting it lightly."

Ros's stepfather, Carter Templeton, was a retired insurance broker, though he still possessed the sternness of the military man he'd been before that. His opinion of Poocheez couldn't be worse than hers.

"It just needs some TLC," she said with the same confidence she'd displayed in countless courtrooms whether she was on the winning or the losing end.

At least before the scandal of her father became public.

Since then, her appearances in a courtroom hadn't been as an attorney at all.

In fact, she'd had to swallow her pride and ask Archer—her stepbrother and Carter's son—to represent her during the seemingly endless grand jury process determining whether or not she'd been an accomplice to any of her father's actions.

She tossed her braid over her shoulder. "I could come for dinner on Sunday," she suggested abruptly, and felt her mother's surprise in the silence that followed. "Unless you've got other plans."

"Sunday is perfect," Meredith said hurriedly.

"About two?"

"Yes, but come as early as you like."

Ros closed her eyes. The delight in her mother's voice was palpable. And painful.

For all of Ros's life, her mother had tried to scale the wall that first Martin and then Ros herself had built between them. The wall had been knocked down a block or three in the past year, but it hadn't been demolished.

Ros was too much Martin's daughter.

Or maybe she just wasn't enough Meredith's.

When her parents split, Ros had only been a toddler. Martin had never remarried. But Meredith had married Carter, the man for whom she'd left Ros's father. Carter already had two children—Archer and his younger sister, Hayley. Then he and Meredith had rapidly produced the triplets—Maddie, Greer and Ali.

They'd been the perfect family.

And Ros had never been part of it no matter how many weekends she'd been forced to spend with them.

She knew a lot of that was her own fault, but now, at thirty-six, she didn't really know how to change it. Or if she even wanted to change it.

Meredith had chosen a life for herself that hadn't included Ros. It was a simple fact.

"Ros? Are you still there?"

She rubbed the bridge of her nose. "Yeah. Sorry." She'd been too lost in her own thoughts; she had no idea what her mother had been saying. "I'm here. I'll see you on Sunday." It was only Wednesday. That gave her plenty of time to get herself in the proper frame of mind.

"See you then, sweetheart."

Ros quickly ended the call and looked over at the refrigerator.

She'd made the mistake of opening it and had nearly vomited from the smell. It had been even more appalling than realizing a possum had run between her legs.

Now she had to figure out how to get the refrigerator *out* of the house and dispose of it. She was sure she'd heard somewhere that the doors should be removed from refrigerators when they were put out to pasture so some curious person didn't try hiding inside and find themselves unable to get out.

Any life-form with a sense of smell would never want to get in that thing, so maybe she didn't need to worry about it.

She propped her chin on her hand and surveyed the kitchen around her. Despite the grime on the exterior of the ancient range, the inside of the oven had been mercifully clean. Once she'd wiped off the layer of dust, it had actually looked as if it had never even been used.

It was likely to stay in that state, given her lack of skills when it came to the kitchen.

She'd pulled the drawers out of the cabinets and taken them outside to scrub down with bleach. Then she'd hosed them off and left them to dry in the sun.

She'd given every inch of the kitchen similar treatment. There was nothing stylish about the room but at least now it was one clean space in this quasi-hovel that she'd purchased.

The same could not be said of Ros.

She was sweaty and covered in filth.

The screen on her phone told her it was nearly five o'clock. Her appetite had been ruined by the possum and the work of the day, but now, the hollowness of her stomach was almost painful.

She needed to go in search of food.

And more cleaning supplies.

But first, she had to deal with herself.

She might have given up every speck of her old life, but that didn't mean she intended on going into town looking the way she did.

She rose and went through the living area that smelled dank despite the aroma of bleach drifting from the kitchen and pushed open the heavy door to the grooming suite.

When she'd explored everything after Trace Powell had left, she'd been very relieved to see that he'd been right. The grooming area wasn't so bad.

Not only was the storage room jammed with supplies and boxes that would take her days to organize, but there were the normal kinds of things she'd expected to see at a dog groomer's business. Clippers. Scissors. Leashes. They weren't kept in a particularly orderly way, but at least they were there. A grooming table. Several kennel cages. A washer and dryer that—thank heavens—proved operational when she tested them on the towels that she'd found in a heap next to the dog washing station.

And though the walls needed a scrub and a fresh coat of paint, nearly every other surface in the grooming studio was covered in stainless steel and therefore easy to clean. *And* there was a bathroom.

Sure, it only possessed a toilet and sink, but it was

in much better condition than the bathroom on the living side of her new digs.

That possessed a shower, but she didn't have the energy to deal with the suspicious mold growing in every corner, much less the toilet that defied description altogether.

She'd yanked the sliding door shut on the whole mess. There were only so many disasters she could deal with in a day.

Now, she approached the wash station with a speculative eye.

The setup was more complicated than what she'd used all those years ago at the animal shelter. This one had multiple gauges and hoses.

But it had more to offer than the kitchen sink.

She looked across the room at the front window. She couldn't even see out the dirty glass between the yellowed posters. Shc turned back to the wash station, bending close to study the markings on the dials.

After several minutes experimenting, one of the hoses finally emitted a weak stream of cold water. No amount of fiddling with the various handles seemed to change the pressure but she did strike it lucky on the temperature.

She went back into the kitchen and flipped open one of her suitcases stacked on the table. She found her cosmetic case and returned to the wash station. The big rectangular tub stood about two feet off the floor with steps for larger dogs to walk up and through the narrow door that swung open and closed.

She stripped down to her bra and panties, pushed the steps out of her way and used the corner of one of the freshly laundered towels as a washcloth. Then she leaned over the side, and by the time she managed to rinse the suds from her hair, she was drenched to the skin and water had pooled all over the concrete floor.

So. Next time, just climb into the damn dog bath altogether. Lesson learned.

She turned off the water and stripped off completely, leaving her underwear in a sopping pile. She wrapped one big towel around herself, another around her hair and returned to the kitchen wearing her wet, squishy sandals.

The gangly ginger-haired boy standing next to the table startled her as much as the possum had earlier. "What the hell!"

He seemed equally as startled, his cheeks turning red, making the freckles across his nose stand out. "S-sorry!" His eyes darted frantically around the kitchen as he avoided looking at her. "My, uh, my—" He thrust out the plastic bag he was holding. "This is for you."

She kept her hands clamped over the towel wrapped around her breasts. She could feel water dripping down her legs. "What is it?"

"Sandwich and apple pie." He chewed his lip and finally set the bag on the kitchen chair closest to him. "My dad thought you might want some food."

"Who is your dad?" Though, now that her heart had started beating again, she figured she knew.

The kid's eyes skittered to her and away again. "Trace Powell?"

Trace hadn't mentioned a son, but then he hadn't mentioned a whole lot of anything. "Are you sure?"

The boy's eyebrows tugged together. "Huh?"

"You sounded like you weren't certain."

Now he was eyeing her as if she had a couple of screws loose. Maybe she did.

She exhaled and found a smile somewhere as she stuck out her hand. "I'm Ros Pastore. And you are—"

He watched her from the corner of his eyes as he shuffled closer, extended his hand and pumped hers twice. "Drake." He let go of her hand and quickly backed away to the doorway.

She had to give the boy credit. He had a firm handshake. And he was doing his level best not to gawk at the screwy lady in a towel.

But then his name sank in.

"*Drake.* Drake, as in—" she looked over her shoulder through the living area to the opened door to the grooming studio "—the Poocheez dog groomer Drake?"

He smiled suddenly, showing off his mouthful of uneven teeth. "You *do* know about me. Grandpa said he'd be sure to tell you but my dad—" he shook his head "—well, he warned me not to get my hopes up that I'd still get t'work here. 'Cause, you know. People like to choose the people they hire. Not, um—" he looked thoughtful "—inherit, yeah, that's what he said. Not inherit them."

Ros's head was pounding again. She'd thought she was "inheriting" a qualified dog groomer. Or at least one she could legally keep on the payroll. "Who is your grandpa?"

"Seamus Shaw. I'm named after him. Seamus Drake Powell. He's my mom's dad. But *my* dad said two Seamuses was one too many so everyone calls me Drake."

Trace hadn't mentioned that "ol' Seamus" was his father-in-law, either. He also hadn't been wearing a wedding ring.

Not that married men were required to do so. And while she knew there were many valid reasons why people—men, women, married or not—didn't wear rings of any sort, she'd always found it personally suspicious when a married man chose not to do so.

He hadn't even possessed a tan line to mark the occasional presence of a ring.

And he'd flirted.

Sort of.

She pulled the towel from around her head to drape it around her bare shoulders.

But now wasn't the time to be inscribing Trace's name in the official Jerk Book. She had the freckle-faced boy in front of her to deal with.

"How old are you, Drake?"

He puffed up his thin chest beneath his faded red

T-shirt. “Eight. Nearly nine.” His throat worked. “Ma’am.”

She’d gotten what she’d paid for and her life was presently reduced to bathing in a dog tub. But the kid’s beaming face was almost enough to counteract her renewed headache.

It wasn’t a person’s fault who his father was, after all.

“Call me Ros. Nearly nine,” she mused. “How near?”

“Five months.”

She studied him seriously until she mastered the urge to smile. “That is very close indeed. And how long have you been a professional dog groomer?”

“I’m not *professional*,” he said earnestly. “I’m just a kid. But I know a lot.”

If the boy knew how to work the dog bathing system, it would be at least one mark in the win column because she wasn’t certain at all that she’d be able to replicate her initial success finding hot water. “Well, Drake, you know there are laws when it comes to employing children.”

His chin started to droop. “That’s what Dad said, too. He said I could work in the family business, but prolly not for someone else.”

The laws were a little more specific but he had the gist and she nodded.

Drake looked over his shoulder outside the doorway. Then he turned back and lowered his voice. “I already gotta do chores for my allowance but that's only five dollars a week."

"Your bills are greater than that?"

He squinted. "I don't got bills. I'm a kid."

She took a moment again to keep from smiling.

"My dad works hard and all on the ranch," he went on, "and the horses are basically just big dogs, but it gets boring 'cause the only thing he lets me really do is clean the barn. Or hold stuff for him." He sounded disgruntled at the very idea.

She swiped a drop of water from her chin. "What sort of work did you do around here?"

He looked confused. "Everything?"

"Is that a question?"

His chest puffed again. "No, ma'am. It's the truth. I gave the dogs baths. I blew 'em out. I cut their nails and I cut their hair. And then I swept up everything and mopped and disinfected stuff."

He did more than she'd done at the animal shelter when she'd been twice his age.

"If you were doing all of that, what did your grandpa do?"

"His crossword puzzles."

She bit the inside of her cheek again.

It had been a long time since she'd wanted to laugh.

"Tell you what, Drake." She hitched her towel tighter. "I can't legally employ you. You're too young."

"S'pose you don't want to do it illegally, either."

She smiled. "Sorry. But I'll try to find some arrangement that still benefits us both."

"Like what?"

"I don't know yet. And I'm not making any promises," she warned.

"I can still come over here and hang out, though, right? I mean, you don't gotta pay me at all. Neither did my grandpa even though he did. I like it here."

What had she been doing when she was eight-going-on-nine?

The answer came easily.

Fighting like cats and dogs with Archer and generally feeling jealous of her mother's other family.

"First of all, your time is valuable so don't be in a hurry to give it away. But as long as it's okay with your dad and you stop calling me ma'am, it's okay with me. However—" she lifted a warning finger "—I have a lot of cleaning to do before I can open for business again. I have to live here, too. So I need to take care of that before I get to anything else."

"Yeah." He wrinkled his nose. "I smell the bleach." He nudged the plastic bag. "It's turkey," he told her. "Dad and I had roast beef but he said turkey was a safer choice on account of you being a girl and all. We kept it cold in the ice chest all afternoon with the container of worms. We was fishing."

"I'm relieved to hear it," she managed mildly. "But—" she raised her brows slightly "—what does 'being a girl' have to do with it?"

"My mom doesn't eat beef," he said, as if that explained it all.

"Sooner you learn that not all girls are the same, the better off you'll be," Ros advised. "And this girl—" she pressed her palm to her chest "—likes beef just fine. In fact, she prefers it."

He smiled happily. "Then next time you can have that. But the turkey *is* good," he added quickly. "Everything they make at Ruby's is good."

"I'm sure it is. And I appreciate you thinking of me."

His freckles stood out again as he flushed.

"Drake." Trace suddenly appeared in the doorway behind his son. He was still wearing his cowboy hat but the sunglasses from earlier were absent. "What's taking you—" His gaze landed on Ros and he raised an eyebrow, looking her over her from wet head to wet toe. "I see."

Her hair hung in tangles down her arms and she was covered from her neck to her knees in thick, albeit dingy, terry cloth. She knew perfectly well that he didn't "see" anything. But she still felt the color rise in her face.

Oh, for one of her designer suits and her power ponytail…

"Go wait in the truck," he told the boy.

"Ros says I can still hang out here."

The father's eyes were darker than the son's. More brown mixed in with the green. And the way they slid over her had her tightening her grip on her towels whether she'd decided he was a jerk or not.

"Does she now?" he asked smoothly. "And it's *Miz* Pastore."

"But she—"

"Truck, Drake."

The boy's shoulders sank. He grimaced and started to slide around his dad to head outside. But he stopped long enough to shoot her a quick grin. "It was nice meeting you, Miss Pastore."

"It was nice meeting you, too, Drake."

Then she leaned back against the counter behind her and crossed one ankle over the other, determined to stare down the boy's father whether she was dressed in towels or not. "I appreciate the sandwich, but it wasn't—"

"And pie."

"—necessary."

"Really?" He glanced beyond the mountain of suitcases on top of the table to the cupboards. It was easy to see they were empty since all of the doors were open, and he couldn't have failed to see the drawers still drying outside. "Stocked up already?" He pulled off his cowboy hat and took a few steps toward the refrigerator, his arm outstretched.

"Stop!" She instinctively stepped in front of him to bar his progress. "You don't want to open the fridge. Trust me on that." She yanked the towel draped around her shoulders back into place when it began slipping. "And as you can see, I'm not really dressed for company."

"Just 'cause someone knocks on your door doesn't mean you have to answer it."

She smiled tightly. "If either you or your son *had* knocked, I wouldn't have. Instead, I keep turning around and coming face-to-face with one or the other of you. How much was the sandwich?"

"And pie. Why?"

"*And pie.* So I can reimburse you."

"Is that how you always respond to neighborly gestures?"

She yanked her towel back up her shoulder again and swiped a hank of dripping hair off her cheek. "When will I get a chance to meet Mrs. Powell?"

"Anytime you want to visit the family graveyard. It's about fifty feet from your kitchen door."

Her hollow stomach cramped. "I'm sorry," she said immediately. Drake had only referenced his mother in terms of Seamus being her father. "I didn't realize."

"If you want to meet my ex-wife on the other hand, you can find her in Braden. Only time she comes out here is if she's picking up or dropping off Drake."

She pressed her lips together. So far, she was really batting it right out of the park. But by keeping her lips shut, the sudden silence felt even more awkward.

That edgy feeling was back again and she realized she was studying the dent in his thick hair left by the cowboy hat. She stepped over to the table and plucked at the thin plastic bag holding the food.

"He seems like a nice kid," she finally offered. Which seemed true and safe enough.

"He is. Do, uh—" He tapped his hat once against his thigh. "I can help you with your drawers."

"I beg your pardon?"

"Kitchen drawers," he said, and she knew then that he did possess a sense of humor.

She just didn't love having it directed at her. Not when she felt so much at a disadvantage.

"I can manage my own drawers just fine." He could take *that* however he wanted. She lifted the wrapped sandwich out of the bag. "Thank you for the sandwich. And—" she forestalled him "—pie."

His teeth flashed briefly and he walked out the still-open kitchen door.

She shivered.

And it had nothing whatsoever to do with the cold water inching down her spine.

Chapter Four

As soon as she turned onto the street where her mother and Carter lived in Braden, Ros wished she'd never told Meredith that she'd come for Sunday dinner.

A long line of cars was already parked at the curb.

She exhaled, feeling ashamed that she actually considered turning around and driving back to Poocheez. Even after four days she couldn't really bring herself to call the place *home* despite the work she'd put into it so far.

She'd spent nearly every waking hour since that first day scrubbing and scraping and hauling. She'd bought an inflatable camping mattress from Shop-World over in Weaver, along with a cheap set of bedding, and set up a temporary camp in the grooming suite.

She was still using the dog bath to wash off because once she'd attacked the mold in the fully equipped bathroom, she'd discovered the pipe in the wall leaked whenever she turned on the shower. But thanks to Drake, who'd come by every day to help pitch in with the monumental cleaning effort, she now knew exactly how to use all the dials and valves for the washing station.

Nobody but her needed to know why she'd wanted to master that particular task as quickly as possible.

She'd replaced lightbulbs, scraped decades-old flyers from the picture window of the grooming suite and shoveled another nest—thankfully empty—from the clothes closet and out to the burn barrel.

She'd dragged the horrible sleeper couch from the living area outside, then tore out the stinky carpet as well because it was disintegrating, anyway—probably because of the water leak from the bathroom.

A salvage truck out of Braden had hauled both couch and carpet away, though they'd refused to take the refrigerator. No appliances, they'd said.

With the room empty, though, she'd scrubbed the concrete floor on her hands and knees until her nails were chipped and her fingers felt raw. But she still hadn't conquered the musty smell. Nor had she addressed the brick fireplace and the fact that she kept hearing something skittering around up in the chimney.

By that Sunday, she had aches in muscles that she hadn't even known she possessed.

She still had to deal with the disgusting refrigerator as well as the deplorable state of the building exterior, but inside, with the heavy door closing off her grooming area at night, she could at least sleep on her inflatable mattress with some measure of ease.

Trace Powell hadn't made another appearance in person, though she had spoken with him once on the phone to verify that he knew and was okay with his son coming over every day.

"Long as he isn't getting in your way," he'd said.

"You don't even know me," she'd said in return. "What if I'm a bad influence or—"

He'd cut her off. "I know enough."

Obviously not.

But she'd let the matter go and that was the end of that.

Drake, who chatted about anything and everything that seemed to enter his head, didn't say much about his father. He just continued appearing each day on a bike with wide all-terrain tires. Then he'd roll up his metaphorical sleeves and, with all of his considerable effort, help with whatever chore was at hand for the next three or four hours. At which point, he'd leave.

When she'd purchased her inflatable mattress, she'd also purchased an inexpensive dorm-size refrigerator to keep some perishables on hand. So far, she'd discovered that Drake could down nearly a half gallon of milk at a single sitting. And he loved peanut butter on saltine crackers and reading the Harry Potter books even more than she did. He'd even chosen to read the third book in the series for his school summer reading project.

She parked her car a block from her mother's house. It was the closest she could get.

As soon as she reached the front sidewalk, she could hear the voices and laughter coming from inside the house and the urge to turn and run grew stronger than ever.

But she was thirty-six now. Not sixteen.

So she straightened the collar of her sleeveless white blouse that she'd tediously ironed with the cheap iron she'd purchased at Shop-World, needlessly smoothed back her tight ponytail and walked up to the front door. Before she could knock, though, the door was yanked inward and her mother stood there, beaming at her.

Meredith had passed on her dark hair and blue eyes to Ros. But that was about it. She had corkscrew curls and was a half foot shorter than Ros, and in contrast to her preference for tailored solids, Meredith wore colorful airy dresses whether it was the middle of summer or the dead of winter. On top of that, she was almost always barefoot and every move she ever made was accompanied by the soft tinkle of bells from her ankle bracelet.

"You're here," she said now, reaching out to clasp Ros's hands. "I was afraid you would change your mind."

"If I'd known you'd called out the masses, I might have," she admitted, bending down somewhat stiffly to accept her mother's quick hug. "You could have warned me you were having the whole family out." Considering the busy lives of her step- and half siblings, she knew it wasn't as frequent an occurrence these days.

"Oh, things just rolled along picking up speed

when Archer and Nell said they wanted to get out," Meredith said blithely. She pulled Ros into the cool interior. "Naturally, everyone had to come to see the new baby."

Ros didn't quite cringe. Growing up, Nell Brewster had been Ros's best friend in the world. When Nell had been orphaned as a young teenager, she'd moved in with Ros and Martin. He'd become Nell's de facto parent. She'd even gone into law herself because of Martin's influence. And after college, she and Ros had still lived together.

But when things had started to unravel for Martin and he'd tried framing Nell for some of it, Ros had sided with her father.

The fact that Nell had forgiven her for her failure of faith was just more proof that her friend had always been a nicer person than Ros had ever been.

She tucked her tongue in her cheek. "So you're saying all the fuss *isn't* about me?"

Meredith lifted her shoulders innocently. "I'll take the fifth on that. No self-incrimination here."

Ros relaxed a little. "I didn't mean to be this late," she admitted.

"Truthfully, your timing is just fine. We needed more ice so Carter and Arch ran out to get it and Ryder fired up the grill a few minutes ago." Meredith was still chattering as she drew Ros into the kitchen, which was almost bursting with people.

"Hey, sis!" Ali—the youngest of the triplets—hopped off the counter where she'd been sitting and grabbed Ros in a quick hug. "How's the dog-grooming life?"

Ros only had the chance to answer, "Not sure yet," before she was accosted by her other two half sisters. The three of them were identical, but they were all such distinctly different women it had always been simple to tell them apart. Ali was a cop and married to a writer. Maddie was a social worker married to the head of a local oil company. And Greer, the eldest of the three by mere minutes, was a lawyer like Ros.

Scratch that. Unlike Ros, Greer was *still* a lawyer.

She was married to Ryder, who—in addition to grill master—was a rancher.

For some stupid reason, an image of Trace swam inside her head and she was glad when someone pushed a plate of nachos into her hand so she could concentrate on something else.

Eventually, she made it through the congested kitchen and outside where Nell was sitting on the porch swing holding the baby. She was laughing at something Hayley was saying, but as soon as she spotted Ros, her laughter died.

Hayley, who'd been a lot less objectionable as a stepsibling than Archer had ever been, gave her a twinkling smile and started off across the lawn toward the grill.

Nell's expression softened and she extended her hand.

Even though Ros had seen her at least a dozen

times now since Martin's disgrace, her throat tightened as she squeezed Nell's hand in return.

And suddenly, she was very glad that she'd come, after all.

She set aside her plate and peered at baby Julia's blissful face. She'd only seen her one other time—two weeks earlier when she'd been born.

"I still can't believe you married my big dumb stepbrother," she whispered before she leaned down to drop a kiss on the baby's forehead. Actually, she *could*, since Nell had secretly been involved with Archer way back in law school.

Nell just hadn't known that Ros knew.

All those secrets were out now, but that didn't alleviate Ros's lingering guilt for her part in breaking up their young, budding affair. It had taken Nell and Archer another decade before they'd found their way together again.

"But I have to admit the two of you did some good work here." She stroked Julia's velvety soft cheek.

Nell beamed. Happiness radiated from her, which only seemed to underscore Ros's lack of it.

She pulled on Ros's hand. "Sit with me. Tell me how things are going with the new place. If I weren't still on doctor's orders to take it easy, I'd have been over to see you by now and help. Carter told us you had quite a bit of work on your hands to make the place more habitable."

Ros carefully sat down next to her on the swing,

not wanting to jostle either Nell or the baby with too much motion. "It's fine."

"Have you met with the former owner yet?"

She didn't want to talk about it. About how she hadn't been able to get in touch with Seamus because he'd left town. "He's in Mexico at the moment," she said. According to Drake, the man intended to build a house on a beach there, no doubt planning to live like a king on the profit he'd made selling Poocheez to her. Drake had innocently provided Ros with his grandfather's phone number and she'd left several messages already to no avail. "What I'm interested in right now is how *you* are doing." Nell had needed an emergency C-section when she'd gone into labor.

"Aside from not being allowed to lift anything heavier than this little girl?" Nell shrugged ruefully. "I'm great. Just a bit sore." She nudged Ros with her shoulder. "I wanted to help you move your stuff from Cheyenne," she said softly.

Ros shook her head. "I told you before. I didn't want help. And I'm relieved that for once everyone actually listened to me." She couldn't keep from stroking Julia's tiny arm. Her skin was so soft. "There wasn't much to worry about in the end, anyway. I sold off everything there was to sell."

Nell sighed heavily. "I wish I could have stopped Martin—"

"Neither one of us could have stopped him," Ros said quietly. Facing that fact was something she still struggled with. Daily. "Look how he tried to frame you on the Lambert estate deal." That was probably the worst thing of all. That when it came to trusting her friend or her father Ros had chosen so poorly. "The man deserves everything he's gotten," she said flatly.

Nell's dark eyes were searching. "Have you talked to him? Seen him?"

"So he can tell me more lies?" She held out her hands. "Can I hold Julia?"

The concern in Nell's eyes was still there beneath the smile. "She's your goddaughter, so of course you can." She shifted and settled the sleeping infant in Ros's arms. "Be warned, though. Holding a baby is a surefire way to get the wannababy hormones surging."

She gave Nell a look over the infant's head. "I don't think it's the wannababy urges that got you in the family way. It was just good ol' garden variety urges that did that."

"Archer's a lot more than garden variety," Nell said mischievously.

Ros rolled her eyes. "Gag. I shouldn't have even brought it up."

"One of these days, you're going to meet a man who gets your urges going," Nell warned on a laugh. "And I don't mean a milquetoast like you usually go for."

"I suppose that's a reference to Jonathan." She shifted, then held her breath when the baby screwed up her face, looking like she might wake up and wail, which is what she'd done the first time Ros had held her. "He had his uses." Their relationship had been something to focus on when her friendship with Nell had felt fractured for good.

"Sure. He liked to cook and he never challenged you on anything. Nice guy but a wimp."

Trace's image swam in her mind. *He* wouldn't strike anyone as a wimp.

She ruthlessly banished him from her mind.

The baby wrinkled her face even more. Her little bow mouth started to open. "Time for your mama mojo." Ros hurriedly nudged Julia back into Nell's arms.

Nell chuckled. "Coward." She jiggled the baby and Julia immediately quieted.

"Absolutely," Ros agreed, sliding off the swing as carefully as humanly possible considering her aching muscles. When the swing still swayed back and forth, she grabbed the chains to stop it.

"You're as bad as Archer," Nell said wryly. "We're not made of glass."

"As much as I dislike the notion of having anything in common with my stepbrother, we both love you. So you'll have to put up with a little protectiveness, I guess."

Nell's eyes suddenly shimmered.

"Cut it out," Ros chided. "Neither one of us is the crying type."

"Hormones," Nell said on a slightly choked laugh. She swiped a finger under her lashes. "Now. Seriously. Tell me about Poocheez. Is it as run-down as Carter claims?"

"I don't know what exactly he's said, but my first afternoon there did involve a possum running through my legs. It was nesting in the kitchen."

Nell's eyes widened. "What did you do?"

"Besides scream?" Ros actually found herself smiling. Perhaps the last few days of grueling labor had put things in perspective. "Not much to do. Trace shoveled up the nest and dumped it in the burn barrel."

"Trace?"

"The neighbor." She brushed nonexistent lint from her black silk capris. "He was there dropping off the extra key to the place."

Nell's expression didn't change, but there was a wealth of curiosity in her simple "Oh?"

Ros looked over her shoulder toward the grill. Ryder was shaking his head and holding a set of long-handled tongs out of Hayley's reach while her husband looked on, laughing. Their little girl clambered on the garden bench nearby.

"Everything's shaping up," she said. "Though I need to figure out how to get rid of a refrigerator that smells like it has toxic waste inside."

Archer appeared with a bag of ice in one hand and a six-pack of beer in the other. "What's toxic?"

"Nothing."

"Ros's refrigerator," Nell provided.

"This is a surprise? It's the natural result when you attempt anything in a kitchen, isn't it?"

Ros rolled her eyes and slid one of the bottles out of the cardboard pack. "I've decided to tolerate you," she told him, "seeing how you were slightly involved in my goddaughter's existence."

He spread his hand across his chest. "I'm deeply touched."

"In the head, but that's something I've known most of my life." She twisted off the cap and toasted his silent laughter with the bottle before taking a sip. She wasn't a huge fan of beer, but it was hot outside and the bottle was cold.

"She needs help getting rid of it," Nell said.

"The toxic waste?" Archer passed the rest of the six-pack off to Greer when she trotted by in the wake of her two toddlers.

"As well as the fridge that contains it." Ros realized Ali had confiscated her plate of chips as she chased her toddler, who was naked except for the cowboy boots on his feet. She studied Reid's little bare butt as he darted away from Ali whenever she got too close. "Do we need to worry that there seems to be an exhibitionist in the family?"

"Some would worry more about the fact that there are four lawyers in the family." Ali grinned over her shoulder at them.

"Three," Ros corrected.

"Only because you're as stubborn now as you've always been," Archer countered. He dumped the ice into the insulated ice chest. "You were cleared of any involvement in Martin's schemes. You could hang out your shingle any time you wanted instead of going through with this whole dog thing."

"This *dog thing* is my future." Ros's nerves were tightening up again and, once more, she wished she hadn't said anything. *"Anyway."* She tossed her ponytail behind her back. "I thought if I could borrow a dolly, I'd have better luck maneuvering the fridge out of the house."

"Maybe Trace has one," Nell suggested a little too smoothly.

Meredith rounded the swing just then. "Who's Trace?" She took the spot next to Nell that Ros had vacated.

"Rosalind's neighbor," Nell provided.

"You talking about Trace Powell?" Carter had followed his wife outside.

"Does everyone around here have to know everyone around here?" she asked nobody in particular. In Cheyenne—before the scandal at least—there was little chance of running into someone you knew every time you turned a corner.

"Handled the insurance on the Bar-H when he came back."

"From where?"

"Marines." Carter leaned over to scoop up ice in his plastic cup, then straightened. "Serving overseas. He came home after his mother died."

Ros had noticed the little graveyard not far from her back door. The overgrown weeds hadn't entirely obscured the headstones but she hadn't taken time to go close enough to read the inscriptions.

"Been working the ranch ever since," Carter added. "Trying to restore it to what it used to be. Helen had left the place in a bit of a mess before she died. Must be six or seven years now." He filled his cup with lemonade from one of the pitchers sitting on the picnic table and grimaced a little as he looked over at the gaggle of children chasing each other around on the grass. Not a one of them was older than four. "Y'think one of these days Reid's going to decide clothes aren't so bad? Kid's peeing on that old garden gnome of yours, Meredith." He looked back at Nell. "Least we won't have to worry about that with little Julia."

Meredith laughed. "Ali hated clothes just as much at that age," she reminded him as she stood up. She kissed his chin and she made her way around him toward the grandchildren. "Ryder, hurry up with those burgers, honey, or we're going to have a revolt soon."

Ros looked down at her beer, very aware of the way Carter's gaze followed Meredith. She suddenly felt right back on the outside looking in again.

She played her part for the rest of the afternoon, though, through the casual but chaotic meal and even stayed until the mass exodus of siblings began. But as soon as Nell and Archer drove out of sight, she left, too.

She stopped at the grocery store to replenish her

supplies. The variety of goods available wasn't as vast as Shop-World, but she wasn't going to drive thirty miles into Weaver just to drive fifteen miles back again to her place. At least she found a nice bottle of wine, which was a plus.

As she turned off the highway, she wondered how long it would be before she could look at the little, run-down building at the end of No Name Road and feel a sense of coming home. Then she had to wonder how long it had been since she'd felt that sense at all.

Even the condo she and Nell had leased for years in Cheyenne hadn't been homey. Ros had spent far more time at the office than she had at the condo. She hadn't expended much effort decorating the place but had simply hired the interior decorator her father had recommended. The same decorator who'd handled the law firm. And the brief stint she'd spent living with Jonathan didn't count for anything at all.

She parked in front of her building, eyeing the ugly homemade sign.

"Stop feeling sorry for yourself," she muttered.

Then she carried her purchases around to the back because she still hadn't found an affordable locksmith to deal with the jammed lock at the front.

She went into the grooming area, wedged the jug of milk into her new dinky fridge and returned to the kitchen. The drawers were back where they belonged. The cabinet doors were shut. She opened one and looked at the bare shelves inside.

"Pathetic," she muttered. She'd had a lucrative career and now she didn't even own a proper dinner plate.

Not that she could cook anything impressive enough to warrant a dinner plate, anyway. Her skill was basically limited to microwavable meals.

And a person needed a microwave for that.

With her limited budget, she'd chosen to buy a blow-up mattress instead of a cheap microwave.

She removed one of the two stemmed wineglasses she'd purchased at Shop-World. They were a far cry from fine crystal. But for two whopping bucks, they did the job well enough.

The only times she'd ever turned on a real oven hadn't gone well, but she could uncork a bottle of wine with her eyes closed. She opened the merlot and carried her glass of wine back outside.

The hot afternoon had turned into a pleasant evening. She sat down on one of the lawn chairs Drake had dragged out of the storage room. The webbing was worn but seemed sturdy enough and she'd decided to leave them both there at the back of the house where she had a view of the rocky terrain and distant mountains. She looked in the direction where Drake always rode his bike. It gave all-terrain bicycling a new meaning.

He'd told her once that if she set out at a forty-five-degree angle from her kitchen door she'd eventually reach the Bar-H ranch house, but she didn't really have a concept how far away it was actually located.

And she wasn't curious, she told herself, closing her eyes.

It seemed painfully silent, sitting there alone as she sipped her wine. But the longer she sat, the more she realized it wasn't really quiet at all.

Insects buzzed. Birds called. If she listened closely, she could hear the sound of water gurgling quietly in the creek.

She tried to empty her mind, but the only thing she succeeded in emptying was her wineglass.

She couldn't stop a soft groan as she pushed out of the creaking lawn chair. She refilled her glass and wandered toward the graveyard.

A low wrought-iron gate, mostly rusted and falling off the hinges, marked the entrance. She pushed at it with her hip until it creaked open.

She yanked down the vines growing wild on the fence and stepped over them, working her way around the brambles and weeds springing up among the weathered headstones. There were only a dozen or so. The giant cottonwood standing in the center of the small plot had protected them to a degree, but a broken limb had caused its share of damage on its way down. Now, the decaying log was a host for two squirrels who popped out of it when she neared. They darted over the wood, fluffy tails quickly disappearing into the brush again.

"Not as alarming as a possum, are they."

She jerked and looked over to see Trace standing on the other side of the fussily filigreed and spiked fence. "You nearly made me spill my wine."

"Sorry." He didn't particularly look it. He pulled off his hat and yanked the gate open a few more inches, which proved too much for the hinges altogether because the gate came off in his hand.

He grimaced and propped it against the fence.

Ros sipped her wine. "Where'd you come from?"

"The very long-ago twinkle in my daddy's eye." His boots crunched through the heavy undergrowth as he approached. "Came by earlier but you were gone."

Today his shirt was navy blue, but everything else about him—jeans, cowboy boots, cowboy hat—was the same. "Why?"

"Why were you gone, or why did I come by?"

She gave him a look.

His smile flashed briefly. "Drake insisted I should see the product of all your efforts this week."

Drake. Of course. She cradled the glass once more against her chest. A squirrel bobbed over a bush and disappeared. "Where is he?"

"With his mom." Trace pointed at the headstone. "Hiram Powell. My great-grandfather." He pointed at the one next to it that was nearly obscured by the log. "Ingrid. My great-grandmother. The first of the Powell wives to be buried here."

She rubbed her thumb along the thin edge of her glass. She felt a little heady, even though she hadn't made it to her usual two-glass limit just yet. "And the others?"

He stepped over the log and held out his hand.

She hesitated for a moment but took it only long enough to gain her footing until she got to the other side of the rotting log. Then she quickly tucked her hand in her pocket and sipped her wine again as she followed him.

"Carolina. Myron." He gestured. The headstones were shorter and wider, and matched each other. "My grandparents."

He turned left and took a few long paces. "Douglas and Helen." He swiped the dried leaves off the top of the single headstone bearing both names. "My parents. He died when I was seventeen. Another seventeen years and she followed him."

Ros read the dates engraved in the granite. Just as Carter had said, Trace's mother had died six years earlier.

"I'm sorry."

"Why?"

"You're too young to have lost both your parents."

His gaze slid her way.

Something light and tantalizing danced down her spine and she looked away. Then she damned the torpedoes and drained her wineglass before turning to face him. "Does it bother you that your family cemetery is located on my property?"

"What do you think?"

"All of this *used* to be part of the Bar-H," she concluded. "So I'll hazard a yes."

He spread his arms. "Hiram and Ingrid homesteaded right here. They built their house where Poocheez stands now." His arms fell back to his sides. "It burned down long before my dad was born."

She winced. "How did the land end up in Seamus's hands?"

"My mother sold it to him fifteen years ago."

"Why?"

Trace's expression didn't change. "I was gone and she thought she needed to."

It was conceivable that he couldn't afford to buy it back when Seamus put it up for sale. "Land rich and cash poor" was more than just a saying. But asking him about it outright felt like crossing a line she didn't want to cross. For both their sakes.

Her little island surrounded by Bar-H land wasn't much and it had cost all she'd had left after paying off the legal fees and the debts incurred by her father's firm. There'd been employees to take care of. Restitution to be made.

Martin had caused the problem but it had been up to her to make things right as well as she could.

If Trace Powell wasn't even more cash poor than she, it ought to have been simple enough for him to reacquire the handful of acres that Seamus Shaw had put up for sale.

But he hadn't. And now it was too late.

She was staying put for the simple reason that it was all she now had.

She continued studying his bearded profile as he looked at the headstone. "I don't like beards." She was appalled that the words actually emerged from her mouth.

"Then it's good you don't have one." It was obvious he didn't care what she liked or didn't like.

He ran his palm down his beard. Which only made her wonder—again—how soft it was.

"I apologize. That was rude."

"Then why'd you say it?"

She opened her mouth, but words failed her. She exhaled and shook her head, annoyed with herself.

Then, instead of saying good night and leaving him to his peace in his family's resting place, she made a point of tipping her empty wineglass out onto the ground. "I still have half a bottle of merlot left." She turned to make her way back to the small iron gate. "If you're interested in sharing it."

Chapter Five

Should I join her?

Trace watched Ros retreat through the overgrown brush.

Sherry wouldn't be dropping off Drake for at least another hour, which left Trace with no real reason he had to get back to the ranch house right this minute.

Whether or not he should stay, though, was a different nut to crack.

He looked around the graveyard. Seamus had left the place to grow wild. Deliberately.

Same as he'd refused to sell the land back to Trace for a fair price.

Instead, the old man had turned around and sold it to a Cheyenne lady lawyer for less than half that fair price.

It was the ultimate up-yours from a former father-in-law who'd never liked him much, anyway.

Trace brushed a last leaf off the headstone and followed in Ros's footsteps. She didn't walk slowly but he still caught up to her easily.

It was hard to tell whether or not she was happy about it as she led the way into the kitchen.

It smelled as antiseptic as a hospital.

Ros had scrubbed the walls back to their original near-white color. Even the tiny blue flowers were visible in the otherwise brown linoleum floor.

"I always wondered what Seamus was thinking when he put that floor in," he murmured. "It was ugly as hell even back then. Sure you're not gonna miss the layer of dirt that covered it up?"

She smiled faintly as she pulled a second wineglass from the cabinet he could see was otherwise empty. "Quite sure." She filled both glasses and handed the clean one to him.

"What do we toast to?"

"Sundays in July?" She barely grazed his glass with her own before she set it aside on the counter and went into the living area. "Come on and see the rest, then. Drake's going to expect that report."

"True enough." He followed, taking his wineglass with him. "Drake told me you pulled out the carpet. I'd have done the same thing."

"Does he spend every Sunday with his mother?"

"When I have him in the summer." His boots sounded loud in the empty concrete-floored room. "During the school year, he comes to me on most weekends."

"Does that put a crimp in his activities?"

"With friends, you mean? Sports? That sort of thing?" Trace shook his head. "Not really. He's playing soccer right now as a matter of fact. But if he has something special going on, Sherry and I can usually work it out."

"Sherry being your ex-wife?"

"Well, she's not my divorce lawyer," he said lightly. Though it was her divorce lawyer she'd been dating when she finally called it quits on their seven-year marriage.

Trace took in the inflatable mattress on the floor. It was about a foot thick and Ros had made it up neatly with crisp-looking white sheets, a plain beige blanket and two pillows. "Wouldn't a sleeping bag be easier?"

Ros glanced at her bed. "Probably, but—" She shook her head slightly and waved at the metal dog bath. "Your son taught me how to work all of that already. He's pretty impressive for an eight-year-old kid."

"He is." Trace noticed the minifridge with an old lamp on top of it as if it were a side table. There was a hardback book next to the lamp but it was too far away for him to see the title. "Wish I could take credit for it."

"Isn't taking credit what dads are supposed to do?"

There was a note in her voice that he couldn't quite pin down. "My dad definitely didn't take credit where I was concerned. Nothing I did met his approval." His father never understood Trace's desire to do something other than work with a bunch of ornery cows day in and day out. "And you've met Drake. He's already his own man."

She smiled slightly. "He helped scrape off the baked-on adhesive from the front window once I managed to peel away the flyers." She went over to stand in front of the window. "Looks a lot better, don't you think?"

He tucked his tongue in his cheek for a second. The sun was angling downward, casting its lengthening rays through the glass and rendering her stark white blouse transparent enough to see the lines of her slender torso. "Definitely got a view now."

She raked her fingers through her hair, releasing it from its clip, and the deep brown strands slid silkily around her arms. "Straight down No Name Road. Who gives a road a name like that?"

"Seamus Shaw," he said dryly. "He's the one who put in the road. Didn't exist before then."

She faced him once more and leaned back until she was propped against the low, wide windowsill. The sunbeams made it difficult to discern the expression in her eyes. "Your mom sell to him before or after you married his daughter?"

When it came down to it, he preferred directness. He just wasn't all that used to it from most women. "Before. But that's actually when Sherry and I met."

He'd been twenty-five, home between deployments and a lot more interested in the comely attractions of Seamus's daughter than he'd been in the man who'd bought a little piece of the Bar-H. "We got married a short while later."

Ros worked one foot around in a circle in the flat leather shoe that looked vaguely like a ballet slipper. "So you're a sweep-her-off-her-feet type."

He followed the line of her narrow ankle up to the edge of her close-fitted black slacks. Everything about her was a contrast in black-and-white. Her hair. Her clothes.

The only color came in the startling blue of her eyes.

"She got pregnant," he said abruptly, even though he'd had no intention of saying anything like that at all.

"So you—" she sketched mocking quotation marks in the air "—did the right thing?"

"The honorable thing."

"Now you sound like my stepfather," she murmured. "He was only in the army for a few years before he married my mother, but the aftereffects have lived on. But—" she abruptly straightened from her perch and brushed her hands together "—I've come to find out, there are worse things." She passed him again on her way toward the living area. "A sleeping bag would have been a temporary measure," she said. "Real bedding is a reminder of my intention to stay."

Talking about anything related to her bed was dangerous at best.

But hell. He'd survived danger before. And even returned to it time and time again.

Which was the reason why he couldn't really blame Sherry for moving on. She'd wanted someone who'd stay. Not someone who kept leaving and might not make it back.

Which just proved that what was honorable and what was right didn't always go hand in hand.

And he could now honestly say he was sorry that she still hadn't found the right man. Neither the divorce lawyer, nor any of the other guys who'd followed, had worked out. Maybe now that Sherry no longer had Seamus living in her apartment as he'd done for the last few years, she'd have better luck.

He swallowed half the contents in his glass and followed Ros back into the kitchen. "Then why not a real bed, too?"

"Air mattress was a fraction of the cost. I bought this place furnished, but Seamus's ad didn't say you needed a hazmat suit to use said furnishings. So now I find myself in the unenviable position of needing to watch every cent until I start bringing in some money again."

"Which you figure the dog-grooming business is going to do?"

"I read the financials. Seamus was making a profit. Not a big one, but still a profit."

"If you say so."

"I'm a simple girl," she said loftily. "I don't need a lot."

He couldn't let that one pass. "Pretty sure there's nothing simple about you."

She shrugged and headed out the door, taking her glass with her.

On the rear side of the building, the light was dimmer. She sat in one of the old lawn chairs and stretched out her legs, crossing her feet at the ankles. "The blow-up bed isn't so bad. As long as I remember to keep my weight distributed evenly so it doesn't capsize, it's more comfortable than you think."

"I've slept in locations that made this place—even before you started working on it—look like a palace." He stood by the chair right next to her, trying to decide whether to sit. But the webbing looked dicey at best.

"You know, you *can* sit," she said as he continued to hesitate. "Despite appearances, I try not to bite these days."

"Not sure that thing'll hold me."

She suddenly smiled. "Is the former marine afraid of putting his hiney through a lawn chair?"

She did have a smile, all right; it melted right through all that chilly gloss. Not smiling back would've been criminal. "Only if the lady's going to laugh."

She gestured at him with her wineglass. "I promise I won't laugh as long as you promise not to sue me if the chair gives up the ghost."

"Fair enough." He dragged the chair around so it faced her and carefully lowered himself onto it. The aluminum frame creaked slightly but the webbed seat, faded and worn as it was, still held.

"See?" She'd left the kitchen door open and the light from inside offered enough illumination that he could see the amusement in her face. "That wasn't so bad."

"Who told you about the marines? Drake?" His son spent half of every day talking about Ros, so it wouldn't be a surprise if Drake talked about him to Ros, too.

"My stepfather actually." She slid down a few inches in her seat and rested her glass on the thin chair arm. Her hair streamed down the back of the chair like a midnight river. "He says he knows you. Carter Templeton?"

Templeton had retired, but his insurance firm still handled the ranch. "I know him."

"Did you know he's my stepfather?"

He shrugged. "It's a small world even when you don't live in an area like this. Why do you think I trusted Drake coming over here all the time?"

She sat forward in her chair, her gaze piercing. "What else do you know about me that I don't know you know?"

He spread his hands. "Do you even *like* dogs? Because you're the least likely dog groomer I've ever met?"

She mulled that over for a moment before sitting back in her chair. "It's a world away from law," she said as if that was supposed to explain it all. "And of course I like dogs."

"Ever had one?"

"When I was young. A beagle I loved more than anything."

"You're still young."

She gave him a look. "I can't decide if that's tongue-in-cheek or not." She didn't wait for an answer. "I haven't had a dog in a long time because I was always working. Not very fair to an animal. So what about you? The only thing Drake tells me about you is that you're always saying that any job worth doing is worth doing well. He says that's what you drilled into him when he started helping out Seamus."

He grunted his surprise. "Oh, yeah?"

"I think it's sort of his mantra now when he's scrubbing away grime instead of running around doing whatever most eight-year-olds do on their summer vacation. Doesn't matter how many times I tell him he should be out having fun, he insists on helping however he can."

"Kid makes a dad proud." He cleared the sudden gruffness out of his throat.

She smiled and focused on pointing and flexing her feet for a minute.

He slowly swirled the wine and decided there might be more than just magazine-perfect looks going on where she was concerned.

She stopped twisting her feet around and draped one leg over her knee. Everything about her seemed elegant. Even the way her shoe hung off her toes.

"How long were you in the service?"

He realized he was staring at her slender ankles again and shook himself. "Sixteen years."

"Long time."

"Enlisted straight outta high school."

"Didn't want to stick around on the family ranch?"

He tapped his nose. "Spot on. Made it as far as gunnery sergeant."

"I'm afraid I don't know whether to be impressed or not."

He shrugged, not particularly caring one way or the other.

"And now you're running the family ranch."

"Consider it a sixteen-year detour." He studied her over the rim of his glass. "How long have you been a lawyer?"

"I'm not a lawyer anymore." She uncrossed her legs and rolled her head around on her shoulders. "You didn't want to stick around long enough to qualify for retirement? My knowledge of the military is limited at best, but you're eligible at twenty years, aren't you? Or have I got that entirely wrong?"

"No." He shifted and held his breath when the chair webbing audibly ripped. "Damn," he muttered when the seat still held. But for how long? "I'm sweating this situation here."

She smiled again and pushed out of her chair. "Here." She held out her hand. "I'll switch with you. That's the one Drake usually uses. The seat on mine seems a little sturdier."

Trace set his glass on the short concrete step leading into the kitchen, closed his hand around hers and stood, ending up mere inches away from her.

Heat streaked through him, and the way she seemed to freeze told him she felt the same.

The day they'd met, her nails had been long. Manicured.

Now they were cut as short as his.

He brushed his finger slowly across the back of her hand and saw something flicker in her eyes.

Then she moistened her lips and finally pulled her hand away, taking another drink of her wine as she sidled around him to examine the seat of his chair.

"Looks like only a couple threads went," she commented, and sat.

He settled into his new chair, then picked up his glass but didn't drink. There wasn't much wine left. He knew the bottle was empty. Once he finished what remained in his glass, there'd be no excuse to stay.

"If you'd have asked me ten years ago, I'd have said I was a lifer," he said abruptly. "I intended to stay in the service until they kicked my decrepit old ass out."

"What changed?"

A lot. "I came back because my mother died. But I stayed because Drake was nearly three years old and he didn't know who the hell I was." He rotated the glass between his fingers. "He ran screaming to his mama every time he laid eyes on me."

Ros was silent for a long moment. "Clearly, he got

past that," she finally said. "And you might say you can't take credit for Drake, but he obviously wants to impress you now. He certainly seems to take his parents' divorce in stride."

"Yeah, well, he never really knew us as a married couple, either."

"Oh." Her brows tugged together slightly. But she didn't say anything more. She just took another tiny sip of wine as if she didn't want to finish it off any quicker than he did.

"What?"

She shook her head. "Nothing."

"You're not going to pretend to be one of those women who do that, are you? Honey, I already know you're the type who says something if you've got something to say."

She narrowed her eyes. "And most people—men in particular—don't welcome that trait."

"I'm not most men."

"I'll give you that," she muttered. She crossed her legs again, though he could tell she wasn't feeling as nonchalant as she appeared. "You surprised me. That's all. I assumed your divorce was fairly recent."

"We split up when Drake was a baby."

He could see her mind working. "So when you said your wife got pregnant it wasn't—"

"With Drake," he finished. He shook his head. "She miscarried a couple months in."

"Ah." She gave a nod of understanding. "I'm sorry."

"So was she."

"Not you?"

"I was twenty-five. I was still adjusting to the fact that my new wife was pregnant, and then a few weeks later she wasn't." He made a face. "I was not the kind of guy any man wants to see his daughter marry. Can't blame Seamus. I was a jerk. Reupped for another four years without even asking her opinion about it, and kept right on with my life as if nothing had happened at all. Considering everything, it was a miracle Sherry stuck it out as long as she did." He scooted his chair around slightly and held out his palm. "Lift your foot."

"What?"

He wiggled his fingers, beckoning. "Your foot."

She frowned but slowly lifted her foot.

He took it and slid off the butter-soft leather shoe to drop on the ground. Then he propped her heel on his knee and started kneading the arch.

She made a sound and tried to pull back, but he gently tightened his hold. "Relax."

She didn't. Not judging by how hard she clasped the arm of her chair and the stiffness of her foot barely resting on his knee. "Is this appropriate?"

He couldn't help a half laugh. "Have you promised your size eights to another?"

"Seven," she corrected. But a smile was touching her lips again. "And no. Neither my feet nor any other part of me is promised to anyone. Not my style." She wriggled her toes. "But you really don't have to rub my feet just because I need to buy myself a pair of shoes that provide proper support."

"You don't have any regular tennis shoes or something? Everyone has tennis shoes."

"You'd think. But yoga is barefoot."

"Yoga, huh? How long have you been practicing that?"

She shrugged. "Long time. Anyway, the closest thing I had to athletic shoes were my golf cleats and I got rid of them along with my set of clubs."

"Why?" How many times had he and his buddies teed up rocks on some barren stretch of land just to entertain themselves?

"They wouldn't fit in my trunk with the suitcases," she said in a dry tone that he didn't really buy.

He pressed his thumb against the knot in her high arch and she groaned slightly. "This isn't fair. I need a pedicure, for pity's sake."

He laughed softly and kept up the pressure. "Vanity, thy name is Ros."

"If you're going to call me vain, that would be *Rosalind*," she corrected with an exaggerated drawl. She sat back, toed off her other shoe and propped her foot beside the other. "Go on, then. Knock yourself out. Foot fiend that you apparently are."

He chuckled. "If I'm going to be accused of a fetish, feet—even ones as ordinary and unobjectionable as yours—wouldn't be it."

She leaned her head back again and watched him from beneath her half-mast eyelids. "I don't know whether to be insulted or not. Ordinary *yet* unobjectionable. There's an epitaph to strive for."

"We could talk about the real fetishes, I guess." He was beginning to think he might be on the verge of his first, considering the way he wanted to start at the fine bones of her ankles and kiss his way up from there.

She snorted. "Definitely inappropriate territory." She wiggled her feet. "We barely know each other."

"And yet, I have your feet in my hand." If he kept up the talk, he'd keep the truth at bay. Pretending to dispassionately rub her sore feet was safer than anything else running through his head. She winced when he hit a particularly tender spot in her heel.

"Hurts so good. What a saying." She swept her hand lazily through her hair and eyed his near-empty wineglass. "Looks like we're out of wine. I do have an excellent vintage of milk," she added, "if you're at all like your son."

"You've discovered one of his weaknesses. Another year or two and he'll be packing away a gallon every other day just like his old man used to."

"Accompanied by a veritable vat of peanut butter." Her lips curved in a smile. "Can't really blame him there, though. It's my weakness, too."

"Good to—" His cell phone bleated and he shifted to pull it out of his pocket.

The chair gave a metallic groan and collapsed underneath him.

She yanked her feet away and sat forward.

They stared at each other.

Then she laughed.

Hard.

She leaned her head back and pounded her bare heels on the ground a few times as she practically howled.

It was inevitable, he supposed, that her chair gave a loud *riiip* and her rear end dropped six inches through the chair seat.

She laughed even harder, which only sent her sinking even closer toward the brick pavers.

He disentangled himself enough from the mangled aluminum to belatedly answer his phone. Rolling to his feet, he kicked the chair aside. "On your way, Sherry?"

"Yeah, finally." His ex-wife sounded rushed. "Drake's soccer game ran la—where *are* you? It sounds like you're having a party."

"No party."

Ros was laughing so hard she was wiping her cheeks.

He tucked his phone in his shoulder and leaned over, grabbing her around the waist and lifting her straight up and out of the chair frame.

It took considerable self-control not to keep holding her there against him. But he set her safely on her feet a good arm's length away.

She grinned, wiped the seat of her pants and picked up their wineglasses, which had both tipped over in the melee. Then she went inside the house.

She was still giggling.

"Then what—"

"I'm at my neighbor's. I'll see you in a few."

"Forty-five minutes, tops. I promised Drake an ice cream from the drive-through."

"Drive safe." He pocketed the phone and went over to stand in the doorway.

Ros was standing at the sink, rinsing out the glasses. "You promised not to sue," she reminded.

He leaned his shoulder against the doorjamb. "And you promised not to laugh."

"True enough." She turned the glasses upside down on a towel to dry. "And *that*, folks, is why Ros Pastore needs to stop after two glasses of wine."

"You have a good laugh."

"Do I? It's been a while. I guess I needed it more than I knew." She angled a look in his direction and the light from the bare overhead bulb exposed the tears of laughter on her cheeks. She wiped them away and sent him a smile.

"Drake's on his way home." It would take Trace longer than usual to walk back to his place because of the dark. As the crow flew, it ordinarily took about thirty minutes.

"So you need to go." She picked up the empty wine bottle. "Thank you for your small yet mighty contribution to finishing this off." She dropped it in the trash.

"Next time I'll bring the chairs."

She closed her eyes for a moment and shook her

head, laughing softly. Then she crossed toward him, but only to reach for the door. "G'night, Gunnery Sergeant."

He backed off the cement step. "G'night, Rosalind."

She made a face and closed the door, leaving him on the stoop.

He was pretty sure he was still smiling when he finally made it back to his place.

Chapter Six

Ros woke up the next day with a vague headache from three glasses of wine. But by the time Drake showed up somewhere around her fourth cup of coffee, the headache was gone. She was just vibrating from too much caffeine.

Maybe there was a lesson to be learned somewhere in there about moderation.

"So, what're we doing today?" Drake was wearing a striped T-shirt with a pair of plaid shorts. His hair was sticking out in spikes and his socks were mismatched. The overall effect was endearing.

"Figuring out what to do about the sign," she said.

"You mean the Poocheez sign?"

"Is there another one?"

He shook his head, a serious expression on his face, and she had to squelch the urge to rumple his messy hair.

"Help me get the ladder."

They went over to the storage room and she yanked open the door to survey the mess inside. The ladder was pinned against the wall behind a metal shelving unit that was shoved full of odds and ends. "Let's just pull everything out," she decided.

He shrugged and went to work, just as he always did.

It was a little daunting to realize a kid his age was nearly as strong as she was. Before long everything that had been crammed onto the shelves was spread out on the gleaming concrete floor of the main room.

There was even more stuff than she'd thought. "Your grandpa really did believe in stocking up, didn't he?" Except there didn't seem to be a discernible pattern to the items Seamus had chosen. For instance, there were about a million pieces of scrap fabric that Drake told her were used as bandannas for their doggy clients. But only a handful of paraphernalia could be sold to the doggy owners. And a lot of the stuff on the shelves didn't have anything at all to do with the business.

Drake propped his hands on his skinny hips and cast a skeptical look around them. "I guess he did."

She grabbed one end of the ladder. "Let's get this outside." He took the other end and they carried it back through the kitchen door and around to the front.

"When're you gonna get the front door fixed?"

She propped the ladder against the wall and pushed her sunglasses up her nose. "Soon as the locksmith shows up to fix it." She'd called three places that morning before she'd found one that didn't charge an arm and a leg for the service call once they learned how far out of town she was. "They didn't give me a date because they're fitting me in when it's convenient."

She put her foot on the bottom ladder rung. She was wearing the same flats as the evening before, because they were the most sensible things in her shoe wardrobe. Her other choices were sandals or high heels.

She really needed to get into town to buy some tennis shoes.

"Keep hold of the ladder, okay?"

He wrapped his fingers around the side rails. "My dad could probably fix the door. He can fix most anything."

She'd spent the night before having entirely lascivious dreams about his father in which Trace had fixed her very well.

"The locksmith's already booked." She went up another rung. She'd been on ladders before to hang stuff like original oil paintings—or law degrees—on the wall.

She hadn't been on an eight-foot-tall stepladder.

She clenched her teeth, focused on the wood sign above her and made her feet move. Up. Up. And up again. Now was not the time to feel shaky.

She drew level with the bottom of the rough-edged wood. She hadn't been sure how it was attached to the wall, but now she could see it was fastened with several large screws.

She glanced down, which was a mistake.

The ground was *much* farther away than she'd expected.

She looked up again. At the cloudless blue sky. The top of the cottonwood in the graveyard was visible even from there.

"You okay, Ros?"

"Yep." She closed her eyes for a minute. *Just do it, already. It's only a ladder.*

She opened her eyes again and felt for the lower rung with her foot. As long as she didn't actually look down, she'd be fine. "H-how'd the soccer game turn out?"

"We lost. We always lose."

She found the next lower rung with her toe. "Probably a drag, huh?"

"Kinda."

"Do you like it, though? Playing soccer?"

"Oh, yeah. Sammy Lee's on my team."

"He your best bud?"

Drake snickered. "Hardly. She's supergood. Way better 'n anyone else on our team."

She smiled faintly. "What's the name of your team?"

"Rocket Aces."

"Sounds fierce. How's Azkaban coming along?" From the corner of her eye, she could see the ground, which meant she was nearly there. "What part are you at now?"

"Harry Potter just rode the hippogriff."

"Ah. Buckbeak. Such great characters." The only other person who knew of her secret addiction to Harry Potter was Nell.

"You think regular people ever write books like that?"

She couldn't help smiling a little. "I imagine even someone like J. K. Rowling considers herself a regular person." She made it down another two rungs.

"How come you like Harry Potter so much, anyway? You're almost as old as my dad. He's *forty.*" He said it as if Trace were positively ancient.

She reached terra firma again and leaned over with relief, her hands propped on her knees. "Good to know I'm looking forty," she said, sucking in a deep breath. "When I'm *thirty-six.*"

"I don't mean you *look* old," Drake corrected hurriedly. "And you're just as pretty as my mom. I just… it's a kid book."

She didn't want to admit any curiosity where Trace's ex-wife was concerned. "Kids' book in theory. I was reading them when I was in school, too." She'd spent hours lost in a fantasy world where a mother's love was strong enough to protect a boy even when she wasn't there anymore to do it in person.

"Are you sure you're okay?"

She squeezed his shoulder and straightened. "I'm fine. We need a big screwdriver."

"Grandpa used t'have an electric screwdriver in the storage room. I didn't see it, though." He squinted up at the sign. "Are you 'fraid of ladders?"

She let out a breathless chuckle. "Evidently. A little bit."

"My dad's got lots of tools."

From hardly any mention of his father the week before to three mentions in the span of five minutes.

If she'd hoped to keep the man out of her mind, the universe was having a grand ol' laugh at Ros's expense that morning.

"I suppose I could quickly run to the hardware store." Though fifteen miles one way to Braden or fifteen the other way to Weaver hardly qualified as "quick" in her books.

"Or I could just get one of my dad's," Drake said with perfectly reasonable logic.

Giving in to the idea shouldn't have been so difficult. "Fine," she said after a long pause. "Is it faster for me to drive you back or for you to take your bicycle?"

"Drive," he said immediately.

Naturally.

She retrieved her purse and pulled on a sleeveless tunic over her sports bra. It was hard not to smile at the way Drake scrambled into her car and ran his hands appreciatively over the caramel-colored leather interior.

"Seat belt," she said.

"You sound like my dad." But he strapped it in

place without further argument. “He says your car is real expensive.”

Too expensive. She started the engine and turned out toward the highway.

“Have to groom a lotta dogs to pay for it, I bet.”

Fortunately, the only thing she needed to pay for with the dog grooming were her living expenses. She’d paid for the car outright when her father had made her a partner in the firm. “I need to sell it and get something more practical.” Yet she kept putting it off.

“Bummer,” he sighed, peering hard at the fancy dashboard. “Is that GPS?”

“Yep.” She pressed a button and the screen lit up. Almost immediately, the lines began appearing on the map, along with the symbol denoting the vehicle. “That’s us.”

He pointed at the squiggly line running nearly parallel to No Name Road. There was a blue area between them, evidently representing the creek. “That’s the road to the Bar-H.”

While Drake fiddled with the satellite radio, she drove out to the highway, down a half mile or so, then turned up the graded road with the plain Bar-H sign hanging over it.

No Name Road wasn’t anything to brag about. It was paved. But the pavement was rutted and cracked.

The Bar-H road, on the other hand, wasn’t paved. Yet the fine gravel was packed down so evenly it surpassed her road in every way.

It was farther than she expected, but they finally reached the house. Ros parked next to a big dusty black truck and sat there for a moment, her fingers still clenching the steering wheel.

She wasn't used to her nerves being held in such a grip. Not when it came to a man. It was almost as perplexing as it was irritating.

Drake pushed open the passenger door and climbed out, clearly prepared to go in search of the screwdriver on his own. And why not? This was his home.

Ros swallowed an oath and peeled her fingers away from the wheel, shut off the engine and followed him toward the two-story building.

The ranch house wasn't enormous, and wasn't particularly fancy. There was a steeply pitched log-cabin-type addition with a metal roof and enormous windows. It jutted out from the center, giving dimension and style to what otherwise would have been an ordinary white clapboard box. A covered porch running around the first story completed the picture.

Ordinary yet...unobjectionable.

Entirely unobjectionable, she thought.

She quickened her step and caught up to Drake just as he threw open a door on the side nearest them and ran inside.

She rubbed her palms down the back of her leggings and followed him into what was obviously a mudroom. Several pairs of cowboy boots, both man-size and boy-size, were lying haphazardly around a long wood-plank bench. Thick iron hooks protruded from the wall. Most of them were empty. A dark brown cowboy hat—looking new and undusty—sat on a shelf.

She stepped around the half-zipped school backpack sitting in the middle of the floor and walked into a kitchen.

There was no real reason to expect that she would come face-to-face with Trace at any moment, but try telling that to her racing pulse.

Drake was pawing through a drawer near the refrigerator, which looked a decade newer than her toxic model and twice as large. She glanced over at the big butcher-block-topped island where a newspaper sat near an empty cereal bowl and a thick coffee mug. The *Braden Gazette*. She hadn't seen a local print newspaper in forever.

But then again, for the last year she'd been avoiding news as much as she could.

"This big enough?" Drake turned suddenly with a screwdriver in his hand.

"I don't think so, honey. The heads of the screws looked really big."

He dropped it back in the drawer. "We got more. Come on."

He led the way past an office area and through the great room. One look at the big windows and the vaulted ceiling and she knew they were standing in the addition. From there it was back outside and across to a disconnected garage filled with several dismantled motorcycles, an ancient truck with the hood up and a weight bench with a huge barbell on it.

The walls were covered in sport pennants and vintage posters, most with military emblems or bikini-clad women. Many with both. Maybe Trace was a collector.

Maybe he liked women with eye-popping hourglass figures.

That left her out, for sure.

"Does your dad work on those?" She gestured toward the motorcycles.

"Yeah. Mostly when his friends come over. They're all military veterans like him." He plucked several screwdrivers from a drawer of the workbench that ran the entire length of the far wall. "Like this?"

She nodded, though it was a wild guess since her experience with tools was as limited as her kitchen skills.

Even though she told herself she was grateful to have escaped running into Trace, she couldn't help looking toward the barn in the distance when they headed back to her car.

But she didn't see him or any horses or cattle. Just an endless panorama of rocky hills and untamed prairie.

She started the engine and eased around the truck, to head back to her place. "Where's your dad? What's he doing while you're with me?"

"Fixing fence. Checking cattle. He has to make sure all the spring calves are growing and healthy. Stuff like that."

"Does he have any help?"

"Sometimes he has to hire help during calving and stuff but right now it's jus' me and Festus. His horse," he explained when she glanced at him. "We got a couple more, but he likes Festus best."

She was less interested in the matter of horses than the matter of Drake being left to his own devices so routinely. "What if you need your dad while he's out doing that sort of thing?"

"I'd call him." Drake didn't say *duh*, but the look was there on his face. "That's why I got this." He pulled a small red flip-phone out of his pocket. "He says I don't gotta have a smartphone at my age." He tucked it away again.

She glanced in her rearview mirror. Despite the smoothness of the graded road, dust coiled in the air after them. "You've had a phone on you all this time?"

He shrugged. "He sends me a text when he's done working and I gotta go home."

"What do you do when you go back home?"

"It's summer. Whatever we want. Hiking. Frisbee golf. Dad set up a course last year. And we go fishing a lot. Dad *really* likes fishing."

She thought about the activities her father had foisted on her whether she liked it or not. Chess club. The debate team. Golf. "Do *you* like fishing?"

"Don't you?" He was bobbing his head in time to the raucous music he'd found on the satellite radio and didn't wait for an answer. "It's cool. Sometimes we go to town for lunch. I like Ruby's café in Weaver better 'n Josephine's in Braden, though. Which one do you like better?"

She smiled and shrugged. "Haven't been to either often enough to judge. That apple pie you brought me from Ruby's was pretty delicious, though."

He poked the radio again, buzzing through stations at the speed of light. "What kinda music do you like best?"

"Class—" she began, but then thought twice. Her father had liked classical music. So it should naturally follow that she liked classical as well. "I don't know what I like best," she said instead.

Drake squinted at her. "How can you not know *that*?"

She raised her shoulders again. "What can I say?"

He chortled, shaking his head. "You're weird."

She smiled.

She'd been called worse.

When they arrived back at her place, there was a strange gray pickup parked out front.

"Who's that?"

"Good question." She nosed her car to the shoulder of the road and parked. "Stay in the car."

"But—"

"Until I know who is here, I'd rather you stay in the car. Okay?"

He frowned but nodded.

She pulled her cell phone from her purse and approached the vehicle. She'd been badgered by enough reporters in Cheyenne. If they'd managed to track her down here, she wasn't going to put up with it. "Can I help—"

She broke off when she recognized the people climbing out of the truck, relief mingling with consternation. "Ali. Grant. What, uh, what are you doing here?"

"Heard about your toxic situation," Ali said. "We came to help." As she spoke, Grant lowered the tailgate on the truck to reveal a dolly in the bed. He pulled it out and set it upright on the ground.

"Nell told you," she murmured, sending her friend silent thanks.

"Archer actually," Ali said absently. "Who's the kid in your car?"

"Neighbor's boy." Ros turned and gestured. "It's okay, Drake. Come on."

He immediately popped out of the vehicle and jogged over to them. He took in Ali's appearance. "Are you really a cop?"

Ali's eyes skipped from Ros to Drake. She preened a little in her uniform. "You betcha. Officer Ali Cooper," she introduced herself. "Braden Police Department. And you, sir?"

Drake grinned and shook her hand. "Seamus Drake Powell, ma'am. I thought cops had to be tall."

Ali's eyebrows shot up and Ros didn't bother trying to hold back a chuckle. She wrapped her arm around Drake's skinny shoulders. "Drake doesn't mince words."

"I see that." Ali's eyes sparkled. "You're Sherry Powell's boy." She fluffed her brown hair, with its streaks of blond and purple. "Your mom does my hair."

Small world indeed.

"Drake's been helping me around here since I moved in," Ros told Ali. "Why don't you show Grant around to the back door," she suggested to the boy.

"Ask him what he does for a living while you're at it."

Grant overheard and gave his wife a wry look. "You don't have to go around telling everyone you know."

"I didn't," she retorted.

"Tell everyone *what*?" Ros asked.

Grant waved his arm. "You might as well know," he said, looking resignedly amused.

"Grant sold a new book," Ali said quickly. "Under his own name this time." She beamed at her husband. "It's a young adult fantasy series."

Ros looked at him with surprise. "I was just thinking about your *CCT Rules* series."

Drake's attention was bobbing back and forth between them.

"Grant is an author," she explained. "A bestselling author, in fact. And he's a pretty regular guy."

"Cool!" Drake looked up at Grant with admiration in his eyes. "How do you come up with ideas? Does it take forever to write a book? How many pages does it take to make a whole book? Are you rich and famous?"

To Grant's credit, he took Drake's rapid-fire questions in stride. "Around back you said?" He pointed at the house.

Ros nodded and he set off, rolling the big dolly ahead of him while he answered Drake's questions.

"Cute kid," Ali commented once they disappeared around the side of the building.

"Yeah. Where's Reid?"

"Day care. We just started him part-time a few weeks ago. Gives Grant a chance to focus on something other than being Mr. Mom while I'm on duty. Drake seems pretty comfortable around here with you."

So much for distracting Ali. She shrugged, unwilling to give her bloodhound sister a scent if she could avoid it. "His grandfather is the one who owned this place."

"A dog groomer." Ali shook her head slightly. "Gotta say, Ros. Most people around here seem more likely to wash a dog with a hose than pay a groomer to do it. When's the last time you were even around a dog? Are you sure you know what you're doing?"

She told Ali the same thing she'd told Trace. "Seamus made a profit at it and so will I." But to her own ears, she sounded more confident about that than she actually felt. Particularly considering she still hadn't found any sort of client listing in Seamus's records. "And dealing with dogs is like riding a bike. I just need a few turns around the block to get the muscle memory going again. Which all of you will see when I open for business again. Grand opening," she said brightly. "Last Saturday of the month."

"That's not even three weeks away. Are you sure?"

Ros nodded, knowing that Ali would do a good job of spreading the word, thus making it even more important for Ros to stick to the short deadline.

But what was the point of waiting around until Seamus returned her calls?

She needed to get an income…and the sooner, the better.

"Right now, I need to get that sign down." She pointed at the ladder still resting against the front of the building.

"It is pretty deplorable."

"My thinking, too. So." She eyed her sister's sturdy work boots. "How do you feel about ladders in general?"

Ali snorted. "You're half a foot taller than me, counselor. Get up on that thing yourself. Or is there actually something the Great and Powerful Ros is afraid of?"

"Your mother should have spanked you more when you were a baby."

"She's your mother, too," Ali countered. "Whether you acknowledge the fact or not."

It was the type of comment Ros usually received from Archer rather than the rest of her siblings. "Since when do I not acknowledge her?" she said evenly. "Are you angry with me about something in particular or is this just Archer's influence coming to the surface?"

"I'm just frustrated with you!" Ali's voice rose suddenly. "And *dammit*, this happened last time I was pregnant, too. Couldn't keep a thought in my head without it coming out my mouth."

Ros looked over her sister's trim form. "You're pregnant?"

"Ah!" Ali stomped her foot. "I haven't even told Grant yet," she admitted in a fierce whisper.

Ros made a gesture of crossing her heart. "Mum's the word. Promise." She touched Ali's shoulder. "I don't want you to be frustrated with me," she said softly. "I don't want anyone to be."

"Yeah. I know. Nell tells us that all the time."

Ros was glad that she and Nell were making headway again, but it was humiliating to think her friend's intervention was needed to smooth the way with Ros's own family.

"Thing is—" Ali scuffed her boot in the dirt "—Mom's birthday is a week from Saturday and we want to have a party for her for once. She's always doing stuff for us, but we never get to do this for her. She's always made us promise not to."

"Some people don't like a fuss being made over them."

"She's never wanted a party before because you never would come."

Ros stared. "That's not true."

"Isn't it? And I'm not talking about when we were kids and you were forced to come because of the visitation agreement between her and your dad. I'm talking about since you've been an adult. You never came up from Cheyenne to see her."

"I came up when Greer and Ryder got married," she objected, stung. "And when Nell had the baby—"

"—but did you try to spend time with Mom and Dad? No. And even after Martin finally got his miserable hide pinned to the wall where it belongs, you won't let her *in*. And now you're living just a few miles away!" Ali's hand rested on her flat abdomen. "It just really...bugs me," she admitted, sounding choked.

Ros felt entirely unequipped to deal with a tearful Ali. Of all her sisters, she was the only one with an edge that came even remotely close to Ros's. "If I say I'll come to the party, will you please stop crying?"

Ali gave her an annoyed look and swiped her nose. "I'm not crying."

"And y'all don't call me the Wicked Witch of Ros behind my back."

Ali's lips twisted. "Okay, so maybe I am crying. A little. You can blame the hormones that we're not discussing just yet. But we haven't called you that since we were kids."

"Oh, well. That makes it all right, then."

"Yeah, *well*, once upon a time you were an insufferable thirteen-year-old. We used to try saying it fast three times. Wicked Ritch of Wos. See?"

"You always were a nut," Ros muttered.

"Takes one to know one."

Ros barely heard her because she'd just noticed Trace galloping up No Name Road astride a big blond horse.

And damned if her heart didn't lurch at the sight.

"And by the way," Ali added, "bring a date."

"Please." Her single state had been dissected ad nauseam the afternoon before at their mother's house. "That's the last thing I need."

"Sure about that?" Ali looked pointedly toward the approaching horse and rider. "That kind of man looks like *just* what you need."

Ros ignored her. Tried to, at any rate. At least her sister wasn't a mind reader.

Grant and Drake had appeared around the corner of Poocheez with the refrigerator strapped to the dolly, and at the sight of his father, Drake bolted past Ros and Ali and headed down the road toward him.

"Hey, Dad," he yelled. "Did ya know Mr. Cooper writes books?"

Trace pulled up the horse shortly before he reached Ros's car and swung down out of the saddle. "What's that?"

"Mr. Cooper." Drake practically bounced the rest of the way toward him, still yelling. "He's an author!"

Trace glanced at the three of them over the boy's head. But his faint smile seemed directed right at Ros.

Then he looked down at Drake, the angle of his hat hiding his eyes.

"Oohrah," Ali said under her breath. "Getting hot out here."

"That's the sun."

"It's not even noon yet. That's the steam suddenly coming off you."

It was easier ignoring Ali than it was the fire running under her skin from just that one look he'd given her.

It was a good thing he wasn't a mind reader, too.

"Sherry said her ex was a marine through and through, but that man's cowboy skin looks real comfortable. I mean, he's even wearing chaps."

Ali's tone was dreamy and Ros shot her an annoyed look. "Don't you have your *own* military man to look after?" Before he'd gotten famous writing military thrillers, Grant had been in the air force.

Ali bumped Ros with her shoulder when Drake and Trace began heading their way, the horse following behind them. "You definitely need to bring him to the birthday party."

"For your benefit or mine?"

Ali laughed. "Yeah, you like him," she said under her breath, and Ros wanted to wrestle her sister to the ground as if they were children again.

Trace and Drake got near enough for Ros to make out the boy's words. "And then he said he'd give me an autographed copy of his new one when it comes out."

Trace's smile widened and he glanced at Ros again. "Pretty nice of him." He flicked the brim of his hat as he looked from Ali to her.

She swallowed. Hard. Her heart was doing a weird little jig.

Ali bumped Ros again. "Going to introduce us?"

Her tongue felt unaccountably thick. "Trace Powell. My sister Ali Cooper."

He tugged off his stained yellow leather glove and started to extend his hand, only to pause and rub it down the front of his dusty shirt first. "Sorry. Mite sweaty."

Ali flicked a delighted glance at Ros before shaking his hand. "Nice to meet you."

"Truth is, I think we've met before." He looked amused as he pulled off his other glove.

"Don't tell me. I gave you a parking ticket?"

"More like a whiskey straight up at Magic Jax. Was a while back, but it's not real often we see ladies with turquoise streaks in their hair."

Ali chuckled. "Happily, I don't have to pull shifts as a cocktail waitress these days." She slid her arm around Grant's waist when he joined them. "This is my husband, Grant."

The two men shook hands and Trace nodded toward the refrigerator, which Grant had left sitting next to the truck. "Getting rid of the fridge, I see."

"Grant knows a guy who refurbishes old appliances for families who need them," Ali said.

"I hope he wears a gas mask when he deals with that one." Ros couldn't imagine how the thing could possibly be salvageable. "I can't even tell you how bad it is."

Trace pushed his gloves into his back pocket. "Need help loading it up?"

Grant sized up Trace. They were about the same height. But while Grant had the lean build of a long-distance runner, Trace looked as though he could lift a truck. "Appreciate it."

Trace handed off his reins to Drake and the two men headed over to the truck.

"I wanna help," Drake said, and pushed the reins into Ros's hands before catching up to them.

Ros stared after them, then nearly dropped the reins when the horse shook his long, white mane and it almost hit her in the face.

Ali didn't even try to contain her laugh. "Better get used to horses," she advised under her breath as Ros stepped as far away from the animal as the reins allowed.

Drake had referred to his father's horses as basically being like big dogs, which she considered a big stretch. "What for?"

"'Cause you can't take your eyes off him," Ali said,

coming closer to her again. “Ros and Trace, sitting in a tree,” she said in a singsong, “k-i-s-s-i-n-g.”

Kissing was only one of the things they’d done in her dreams. “You’re out of your mind.”

Ali patted her flat belly and smiled beatifically. “Trust the mama mojo.”

Chapter Seven

Trace watched the pickup truck with the refrigerator loaded in the back drive down No Name Road. One part of his mind was on Drake's constant chatter about how cool it was to meet a "real live" author.

The other part of it was preoccupied by Ros.

She was wearing yoga pants for one thing. Black and formfitting from her waist to her knees. A black sports bra was plainly visible beneath a gauzy white excuse of a shirt. As was the span of skin between the bra and the waistband of the leggings when she reached up to twist her hair into a knot on top of her head.

"You can get it down, right?"

He realized Drake was talking to him and glanced at his son.

Drake jerked his thumb. "The Poocheez sign."

"Why do *I* need to get it down?"

"Ros is afraid of ladders."

"Not ladders, per se," she interjected. She stopped next to the ladder and wrapped her hand around the rung that was at her eye level. "*Falling* from the ladder, to be precise."

"You can get it, right, Dad? We already got the biggest screwdrivers from your tool drawer, too."

Trace had spent the morning herding two dozen head off Double-C land and back onto Bar-H through a stretch of downed fence. He'd secured it the best he could with the limited supplies in his saddlebag, but he needed to drive back out there and set a couple new posts or he'd be doing the same damn thing again tomorrow.

After he'd helped load up the fridge, he'd taken the reins back from Ros, intending to head back to the ranch and get to work.

But now he took in Drake's expectant expression, then looked at Ros, whose face was entirely unreadable. In fact, she didn't seem to want to meet his gaze at all.

After their time together the night before, it annoyed him more than he wanted to admit.

"Sure." He looped Purdy Boy's reins around a tree branch. The quarter horse was the newest addition to the Bar-H and still had enough bad habits from his previous owners that Trace couldn't just ground tie him yet the way he could Festus. "And what screwdrivers?"

"I left them in her car." Drake darted off.

"What I'd give for a fraction of his energy," Trace muttered on a sigh.

"You don't *have* to do the sign," Ros said, clearly inferring that he didn't want to.

"Now would that be neighborly of me?" He pulled

off his hat and swiped his brow with his arm, not waiting for an answer. "How'd you sleep last night?"

She stiffened. "I slept perfectly well."

He moved closer. "That makes one of us, then."

"If it's because of the chair collapsing on you—" She looked down at the boot he propped on the lowest rung of the ladder.

He leaned closer to her, deliberately invading her space just to see her reaction. "What happened to the woman I was with last night?"

"I drank too much wine last night." She still wouldn't meet his gaze and he could see the way she swallowed. But she didn't retreat an inch despite how close he was.

The fact that she stood her ground was aggravating, too. Because he liked it. Respected it.

"A couple glasses of wine might have shown the cracks in your glossy armor, *Rosalind*, but you weren't drunk." He straightened as Drake came back with the oversize screwdrivers. "I know drunk."

At that, she shot him a look, but then Drake stopped next to them and she looked at the boy.

"Here." Drake held up the tools.

Trace took two of the screwdrivers and went up the ladder. The first three screws came out easily enough. The fourth screw head was totally stripped and he finally just grabbed the slab of wood and yanked hard.

The wood splintered with a huge crack and came

loose, and would have flown out of Trace's grip if he wasn't careful.

"No wait!" Ros shouted. He looked down and swore under his breath at the sight of Purdy Boy racing away, the reins trailing in the wind.

She looked up at him. "What should we do?"

"Nothing. Back away." He waited until she'd moved a safe distance and tossed the sign to the ground before climbing down the ladder again. "Purdy'll find his way to the barn like always."

Ros crouched next to the sign to examine it up close. She lifted the edge of the rough plank to look at the side that had split.

Drake knelt next to her so their heads were close together, his ginger hair contrasting with her dark brown locks. "Now what?"

"I thought I'd stain it or paint it but—" She suddenly pulled her hand back and studied her fingertip.

Splinter, Trace surmised. *Shocker.* "Need to square off the bad edges and sand it all down before you do anything at all with it."

"Your dad's right," she told Drake. "But I'll have to get the supplies before I can go any further." She pushed herself upright. "I can drop you two off at your place on my way to town."

"What about my bike?"

"We can put it in the trunk. I won't be able to close it, but it'll be okay for as long as it takes to drive you home." She glanced at Trace, then quickly looked away again. "You took time to help loading up the fridge and this thing—" she pushed the big piece of wood with her toe "—so it's only fair." She waited a beat. "Neighborly. Unless you *prefer* to walk."

"Get your bike," he told Drake, and the boy immediately trotted off around the side of Poocheez.

Ros had gone back to studying her fingertip.

"Let me see."

She hunched her shoulder against him. "It's fine." She turned and walked toward the vehicle.

Her gauzy shirt was just long enough to hit right above her sashaying rear.

He looked away and caught Drake watching him speculatively as he wheeled his bicycle past him.

Trace swiped his forehead again, resettled his hat and followed.

Ros popped the trunk. Trace deftly removed the wheels of the bike, tossed them into the trunk and stowed the frame on top of the wheels.

"Handy trick," Ros said, watching.

"Grandpa drove a car, too," Drake said. "My bike fit in his trunk this way, too." He opened the passenger door and climbed into the backseat while Ros got in the driver's side.

Trace shut the trunk, angled himself down into the passenger seat and then they were off.

He was glad it wouldn't take long to get to the Bar-H. Not even Drake's steady stream of comments about the car's cool accessories was enough to distract Trace from the feel of her shoulder brushing against his every time they hit a bump in the road.

This was why he drove a big, spacious pickup truck.

No matter how he sliced it, his shoulders took up space. It was a simple fact of life.

He was never comfortable in cars.

And this was almost torturous.

He shifted slightly, trying to get his mind off the scent of her. Not easy when the windows were closed and she had the air-conditioning going full bore.

"Will your horse really go back to your barn?" she asked, sounding genuinely curious.

Drake leaned forward. "It's Purdy Boy's favorite place to be. Right, Dad?"

"Yeah." He absently tapped the cowboy hat on his lap and stared out the window at the cattails growing in the creek. "That's his problem. Lazy horse."

"Dad says Purdy's lazier 'n we are on a summer morning," Drake added.

She turned onto the highway. "Can't imagine either of you being lazy. I haven't seen it yet."

Trace glanced at her. "You need to work on your imagination."

For a brief moment, their glances collided.

Then she stared straight ahead again. Her knuckles looked nearly white around the steering wheel; in contrast, her cheeks were rosy.

Regardless of the chinks in her armor, she hadn't struck him as the type to blush.

It was probably just the heat that not even the

air-conditioning she suddenly cranked even higher could combat.

He shifted again, adjusting the hat on his lap. She wasn't the only one who was overheated.

When she pulled up next to the pickup truck at his ranch house a short while later, the wheels had barely stopped turning before he was out of the car. "Thanks for the ride. Drake, get your bike out of the trunk." He strode straight ahead, toward the barn.

He wasn't worried about Purdy Boy. He was just putting some distance between himself and Ros.

A few minutes later, he heard her car retreating. He scooped up water from the water trough, sluiced it around his neck and turned back around again.

He found Drake, tongue tucked between his teeth, diligently trying to fix the wheels back into place on his mountain bike.

Even though it would have been faster for Trace to do it himself, he waited until Drake had accomplished the task. Then he told him to put away the bike and meet him back at the truck.

"Are we going to lunch in Weaver again?"

"I need to set a couple fence posts first. You can hold the tools."

Drake made a face, but he didn't protest.

Trace already had the supplies he needed in his truck, so as soon as Drake climbed up beside him, they set off again, with Trace driving around the barn and cutting off across the rangeland.

"If you married Ros, I could work at Poocheez for her when she opens up again."

Trace was glad he *wasn't* on the road, because he might have driven right off it. "Where the hell did you get an idea like that?"

"I can't work for her like I could for Grandpa 'cause we're not family. But if you—" Drake suddenly grabbed the dashboard. "Jeez, Dad, watch—"

Trace jerked the wheel just in time to avoid a huge sagebrush. "Your grandpa was only paying you a few bucks a week, anyway. If you're hurting so bad for money, your mom and I can talk about increasing your allowance."

"He was paying me seventy-five dollars a week!"

Trace changed gears to head down a steep ravine. "Seventy—" He shook his head. Barking at Drake as though he was a raw recruit wasn't going to accomplish anything.

Especially when what he really wanted to do was strangle Seamus Shaw.

It was a good thing the man had left the country or Trace would've been strongly tempted to hunt him down and do it.

They jolted back up the other side of the ravine, and he bumped to a stop before eyeing his son again. "Seamus had no business giving you money like that. Does your mom know? What have you been doing with it? And why am I just now hearing about this?"

Drake sat there, mutinously quiet. It was a new trait he'd developed just that year.

The truck engine ticked softly and Trace ran his hand around the back of his neck, squeezing the base of his skull in an attempt to ease the pain that had cropped up there. "If you want to work, you can work here at the Bar-H." It was surreal hearing his father's words coming out of his own mouth.

"You don't let me do anything interesting like Grandpa did," Drake muttered. "Just hold tools and shovel horse sh—" He shot Trace a look. "Crap," he amended.

The boy was right. But Trace hadn't wanted his son to feel all the demands of ranching the way Trace had. Growing up on the Bar-H and working the ranch hadn't been a choice for Trace but an expectation. And he damn sure hadn't been paid like a hired hand would have been.

Combine that with two parents constantly at each other's throats, and Trace had felt suffocated until the day he'd left. To this day he didn't know which had been the chicken and which had been the egg—Helen Powell's bitterness with her lot in life or Douglas Powell's love for the bottle.

"Fair enough. Just remember the more I let you do around the Bar-H, the less time you'll have to spend over at Poocheez. So you better think on that pretty good before you get mad at me for letting you stay a kid as long as possible.

"And I'm not marrying anyone," he added flatly.

Drake didn't say anything more and Trace didn't

know whether he was glad, or if he missed Drake's usual tendency to badger a subject to death.

Regardless, he was glad to reach the short stretch of downed fence even if it was to find that, once again, several head of Bar-H cattle were grazing on the other side of it.

He turned off the engine and climbed out. "Come on," he told Drake. "You want to do more, here's your chance."

The boy got out and together they chased the cattle back where they belonged. Then Trace drove the truck closer to the fence line. If the animals kept thinking the grass was greener on the other side, at least the truck would block part of their way.

Then he handed Drake a pair of heavy leather gloves from the truck bed toolbox. "Put those on."

Looking surprised, Drake pulled them on. They were way too big but Trace tightened the wrist straps so at least they wouldn't fall off. He handed him the fence pliers and the bucket of ties and staples he kept stored in the toolbox, grabbed two new T-posts and the post driver from the truck bed and carried them to where the old wood post hung, barely held up by the loose strands of wire.

Evidently Drake's curiosity was enough to break the ice. "How come the wood post snapped off like that?"

"'Cause it's been standing out here in the sun and the snow for half a century or better." He put on his gloves and showed Drake how to pull the looped staples out of the wood, freeing it from the barbed lines.

"What do we do with the post now? Can we reuse it?"

Trace pushed at it with his boot. The wood was weather-beaten and rough, but only the bottom of it had rotted. "If not, we can always burn it." He started to reach for it, but Drake grabbed it, dragged it to the truck and pushed it into the bed.

Trace grabbed the new T-post and quickly set it deep into the ground with the post driver about a foot from where the original had stood. He would've preferred to put in a new wood post, but shoring up the fence with two metal posts would do for now.

"Can I try?"

Trace held the second post upright. It was almost a foot taller than he was. "This thing is seven feet tall. And this—" he held the driver by one of the handles that stuck out on both sides of the long cylinder "—is heavier than you think."

Drake's chin stuck out. "I could do it."

Trace handed him the heavy tool and hid a grin when Drake took a bracing step against the twenty pounds. But he managed not to drop it.

"I'll get the post started and we'll see."

He paced off the distance to the second T-post and drove it down a bit by hand first. Then he lifted the driver over the top of the post and gestured for Drake, who reached up and grabbed the handles.

His face screwed up, he tried lifting the driver so

he could pull it down again, impacting the top of the T-post, which, in turn, would drive the post deeper in the ground.

But he didn't have the leverage to make the thing move at all.

Drake's shoulders fell.

Trace chucked him under the chin. "You're not tall enough, son. But that'll change soon enough." He took over the driver and soon had the post buried nearly two feet deep. Then he stepped back. "Now try it."

Drake grabbed the handles again and pushed upward, then let the weight of the tool drop against the top of the post. After doing that three times, he was breathless and happy enough to call it quits.

He kicked back on the ground watching while Trace traipsed along the fence line tightening up the barbed wire to his satisfaction.

Ranching.

Fifty percent luck.

Fifty percent hard work.

Fifty percent dealing with endless miles of barbed wire.

"This part'll be easier," he said, knocking his boot against Drake's tennis shoe. "These five wires I tightened up now need to be tied to the new posts just like all the old posts. That's what helps keep the wires evenly spaced out and tight enough to do some good. That's what these things are for." He showed Drake the post clips in the bucket. "They attach on this side like so—" He looped the hooked end of the clip around the wire on one side of the post, then the other side. "Grab the clip with these special pliers—" he demonstrated the action "—and twist it up, then over. Then you space the next wire down this far." He measured the distance by the length of the pliers. "And the next clip goes right there. Got it?"

Drake nodded, and with his tongue tucked in his cheek in concentration, he fastened the clip.

By the time they were on the fifth strand of wire, Drake was fastening the post clips like a pro despite his overlarge gloves. But the boy's face was looking sunburned.

Something for Sherry to get on Trace about.

That was okay. He'd just need to start making sure Drake wore one of the cowboy hats that invariably ended up shoved under one of the twin beds in his bedroom.

They carried the extra supplies back to the truck and Drake worked at the strap holding his gloves snug on his wrists. "Grandpa puts it in a savings account at the bank for me so I can go to college someday," he said suddenly.

Trace slowly locked the toolbox and looked down at his son's sweaty head.

Trace's only education had come courtesy of the military. He knew the importance of college, and didn't appreciate Seamus's assumption that Drake wouldn't be provided for. "How much you got saved?"

Drake puffed up his chest. "Two thousand, five hundred and thirty-five dollars."

"That's a lot of dog baths." A helluva lot of them. He opened Drake's door for him, then walked around the truck and got behind the wheel. "Are you already worrying that your mom and I aren't planning to send you to college?" he asked once Drake had climbed up into the passenger seat.

"No, but—" Drake shrugged and ducked his chin as he fastened his seat belt. "It's just what Grandpa wanted me to do. He said he never planned ahead for my mom so he wanted to do better for me. And besides, I like the dogs." He sent Trace a quick look. "But I like tying wire, too. It's *way* better 'n cleaning out the barn."

Trace tended to agree on that. And until about six years ago, he'd never thought he'd ever appreciate the tedious task of mending fence.

Just went to show that everything was relative.

Fresh air. A decent tool to make a job easier.

Things could be a lot worse.

He could be trying to staunch the blood of fellow marines.

He put the thought to bed and the truck into gear. "What d'you think you want to do when you go to college?" he asked eventually.

"I dunno." Drake was pulling at his lower lip, a sure sign he had something on his mind.

"You were pretty excited about meeting a real

author." Drake devoured books in a way that Trace never had.

"Yeah. He's cool. You *like* Ros, right?"

Trace felt a hitch in his gut and he made himself shrug. "Sure," he managed to say in an unconcerned tone. "You want Ruby's again?"

Shameless ploy or not, he didn't want to get in a conversation about their neighbor. Enjoying her company was all fine and good. Spending half the night thinking about her when he should have been hitting the hay wasn't even the worst way he'd ever spent a night.

But he didn't have the energy to wonder which version of Ros she would present the next time.

Particularly when he knew she'd never stick it out there. Especially when he was just biding his time until he could restore her land to the Bar-H where it belonged.

And most importantly, regardless of motivation, Trace didn't need his boy cooking up notions like marriage.

Trace knew what his strengths were and being a husband wasn't one of 'em.

It had taken him too long to be a decent father. Being a husband again wasn't in the cards.

"So?" He reached out and scrubbed his hand over Drake's spiky hair. "Ruby's?" If they didn't dawdle, they could still make it before the place closed for the day.

"You think Tina will be working today?"

Trace gave him look. Tina was one of the regular waitresses at the diner. "Why?"

"She's real pretty." Drake drew an hourglass in front of him with his hands.

Trace couldn't help but laugh.

One more reason to value his time with Drake.

Sooner than Trace would be ready, his son would be grown.

And he'd leave the Bar-H the same way that Trace had.

Chapter Eight

They made it before Ruby's closing time, but barely.

And Drake was clearly deflated when he discovered that Tina had already left for the day.

They took their sandwiches to go and ate in the park where a birthday party was going on underneath the big white gazebo and a pickup game of basketball was in progress on the court.

Drake had barely finished his French fries before he was rushing over to climb on the enormous jungle gym. Trace leaned back on the park bench in the shade and watched Drake clamber on the structure with a half dozen other kids he didn't know from Adam. Which just proved he was still just a kid, whether he'd started saving money and appreciating pretty girls or not.

It was the kind of moment that made Trace wish he could stop and freeze time.

Just for a while.

On their way back out of town, they stopped at the Udder Huddle for ice cream, and when Drake said they should take something to Ros, Trace couldn't come up with a good reason not to. The clerk behind the counter said she could pack their order on ice to ensure nothing prematurely melted.

"Peanut butter topping, though?" Trace looked at Drake. "Are you sure it shouldn't be chocolate?"

"Chocolate's my mom's favorite," Drake replied. "Ros likes roast beef sandwiches better 'n turkey. And I bet she'll like peanut butter better 'n chocolate, too, same as me."

So peanut butter, it was. Trace paid for the sundaes and then they headed back home.

In the general scheme of things, fifteen miles of highway wasn't that far. When it came to the one running between Weaver and Braden, though, that fifteen miles was made of up narrow curves and—in most places—a single lane of it either way.

Ten minutes into the drive, Drake was asleep, his head bobbing over the insulated container he was holding on his lap. Trace gently pulled the container out of Drake's lax grip and set it on the floor. Then he continued the drive in silence until he reached No Name Road and turned off.

Drake didn't even wake up when they changed speed or the road got bumpier. And when Trace parked behind Ros's car, rolled down the windows and turned off the engine, his son just tilted his head back against the seat and started snoring.

Trace pulled the sundae out of the bag and quietly got out of the truck. He was surprised to hear rock music coming from inside Poocheez. He'd figured her for more of a fan of Mozart than metal from an era before either one of them had been born.

That had been the soundtrack of *his* life after he'd enlisted. His first platoon CO had liked nothing more than rock—and the harder, the better. Didn't matter in the least what decade it came from.

Trace followed the sound of '70s-era Nugent around to the back of the building and stopped short.

Her back was turned to him. He noticed that she was still wearing the same clothes as earlier, though the gauzy shirt was gone. She stood at the kitchen table she'd dragged outside, working on the Pooch-eez sign that she'd propped on top.

She was putting her entire body into the effort of working the sandpaper across the surface in time to the heavy guitar riffs of "*Stranglehold*."

Forward and back.

Forward and back.

Every movement highlighted by the clinging black yoga pants.

A thin trickle of ice cream melted over his thumb and he blinked. He licked it away and cleared his throat—loud enough that she'd be able to hear it over the music.

She straightened like a shot and whirled around to face him.

"Surprising choice," he greeted loudly.

"What?"

He lifted his finger in the air as the guitar whined. "Music."

"Oh." She looked toward the open kitchen door. "Drake asked me this morning what kind of music I liked."

"And you like Ted Nugent?"

"Is that who it is?" She listened for a minute, then winced. "Lyrics are—"

"No worse than stuff that's brand new." He held out the sundae. "Here."

She set aside her sandpaper and reached for the clear plastic cup. "Ice cream?"

"With peanut butter topping. Drake was positive you'd prefer it over chocolate."

Their fingers brushed as she took it from him. "I do."

The beat of the music was like a hard, heavy heartbeat between them.

Trace cleared his throat. At least she wasn't avoiding his eyes the way she had that morning. Only now, he kept hearing Drake and his fool marriage talk in his head.

"It's gonna keep melting."

She looked at the cup of ice cream as if she'd forgotten she was even holding it.

"Right." She turned and strode inside and he noticed the brilliant white tennis shoes on her feet.

She'd purchased more than sandpaper in town.

He followed her into the kitchen to find her adjusting the volume on an ancient boom box on the counter.

"I just turned the radio to a station that wasn't all

static. Didn't matter to me what they played." She pulled open a drawer. "It was this or talk radio."

"Need satellite radio if you want to get more choices than that around here." Her cell phone sat next to the boom box, blinking out a fresh notification that she had a number of missed calls. "Wasn't all that long ago that we couldn't even get a signal for a cell phone out here."

She shut the drawer with her hip and stuck the spoon into her ice cream. "Where's Drake?"

"Snoring in the truck. Where'd you find the boom box?"

"It was one of the *many* things we pulled off of Seamus's storage shelves." She walked through the empty living area to the grooming room.

Beyond her inflatable bedroom, crap was stacked in piles from one corner to another.

"Wouldn't you have more room if you moved your blow-up bed into the living area?"

"Yes, but if you stop to take a whiff, you'll note it still smells in there. Plus I think something's living in the chimney, and it creeps me out." She was winding her way through the maze. "Did you know your father-in-law was such a packrat?"

"Former father-in-law," he corrected. "And there were a lot of things I didn't know. Like the fact that the wages—" he air-quoted the word "—he'd been paying Drake were going into a secret savings account."

She peered through the front window at his truck,

with Drake still sleeping inside. "Is a savings account such a bad thing?" She looked back at Trace and sucked on the contents of her spoon.

He looked away only to end up staring at the precisely folded edge of the sheet on her blow-up bed. She could give lessons in military corners. "According to Drake, Seamus says the money's for college so I can't really say it is, can I." He realized his gaze was bouncing around like a pinball in hunt of a safe place to land. But she was always in the frame.

"It irritates you, though."

"One of Seamus's pleasures in life is irritating me. One of these days, he's going to want Drake to go down to Mexico and visit him, too. And it'll be another thing I'll suck up for the sake of my son." He accidently bumped the corner of her minifridge and caught the bulbous ceramic lamp on top of it when it wobbled. Then he noticed the cover of the book sitting next to it. "Did Drake leave this?" he asked, picking it up.

"It's mine. One of my favorites actually." She lifted her chin slightly as if expecting him to say something derogatory.

"You and a bazillion other people. I had a CO once who was into reading that whole Potter series. Claimed it was because of his kid back home but none of us believed it." He replaced the book. "I should get Superboy out there home. It was a busy day."

"Thank you for the sundae."

"Thank Drake. It was his idea."

Her eyes were very blue. "Then tell Drake thank you for me."

If he didn't immediately head out, he was going to do something he knew he'd end up regretting.

"Well." He shoved his hands in his pockets, but he still didn't turn to go. Instead, he eyed the front door. "I could probably take a look at the lock for you."

She was twirling her spoon in the cup, mixing the melting vanilla with the creamy topping. "I have a locksmith coming."

He nodded. Mentally ordering himself to do an about-face, he walked back through to the kitchen and outside. He saw the pack of sandpaper sheets and the already worn-out sanding sponge. It would take her forever to get the wood sign smooth with the items she'd chosen.

"Did you get that splinter out?"

"Hours ago." But she swept her hand behind her back, looking as guilty as Drake did whenever he got up to mischief.

He held out his hand. "Give it to me."

She raised imperious eyebrows. "You're sounding very gunnery sergeant-ish all of a sudden."

"Gunny," Drake said, appearing around the corner of the building and surprising them both. His face was redder than his hair. "That's what they call Dad. From back when he was a marine."

Drake made it sound like it was a hundred years ago.

Trace dropped his hand. It wasn't up to him

whether Ros ignored a splinter or not. Just like it wasn't up to him if she chose the hard way of dealing with that ugly-ass piece of wood. Or if she paraded around in towels or yoga togs or tiaras.

He stepped around the table and the sign and closed his hand over Drake's shoulder. "Get a sanding block," he said to Ros. "And coarser grit sandpaper. You want to work your way up to the fine grit stuff you've got there."

Then he steered Drake toward the corner of the building.

Drake squirmed out of Trace's grip. "See you tomorrow morning, Ros."

"See you tomorrow, honey."

Trace's nerves tightened up like someone had just twisted a fence post clip around them.

Ros did not see Drake the next morning.

Nor the next afternoon.

Not that she needed the boy around to get through her day or anything. But by that evening she was still curious, so she searched through the dozens of missed calls on her phone to find Trace's number from that first night. She saved his name in her contacts and hit Dial.

After several rings, though, all she reached was his voice mail.

"It's Ros," she said in such a rushed way that it was embarrassing. "I didn't see Drake today. Just thought I'd check on him."

She realized she was twisting her hair around her finger as though she were twelve and made herself stop.

"Okay. That's all. Um. Talk to you later." She ended the call and flung herself down on her mattress. But it needed more air and she rolled off it again, groaning a little at her aching muscles as she went to retrieve the electric pump from the storage room.

Without Drake's company, she'd spent the day sorting and organizing the space while the radio blared an incomprehensible medley of music. The end result was a storage room that was the complete antithesis of Seamus's Fibber McGee mess, and Ros being no closer to knowing what kind of music she actually did prefer.

One thing she did know, though, was she'd never be able to hear that pulsating song from the evening before without remembering the look in Trace's eyes. As if he *had* been reading her mind, after all, and knew her every intimate thought where he was concerned.

At least she'd managed to channel her sexual frustration into rearranging the shelves to create an orderly display of useful items.

In terms of the rest of the stuff from the closet, she'd culled anything that might be salable—which wasn't much—and piled everything else outside the building to go to the dump.

She grabbed the air pump and an extension cord

and plugged it in. Once she was certain it was pumping its small but steady stream of air into the mattress, she went into the kitchen and made a peanut butter sandwich. She ate it, sitting at the counter alongside the boom box, since her kitchen table was still outside.

When she heard the air pump automatically shut off, she turned down the volume on the radio for a moment and cocked her head, listening to the silence that wasn't really silence.

The ancient stove had a dial clock on it that ticked audibly. The oscillating fan that she'd bought the day before at Shop-World to help circulate some fresh air through the place hummed with a soft whir. The crickets outside the kitchen window that she'd finally succeeded in opening after cutting through the paint that sealed it shut were in full chirping mode.

She went into the living area and eyed the plain brick fireplace. There was a screen over the opening but if something wanted to climb down the chimney, it could.

At least right now, she didn't hear the soft scratching coming from deep within the chimney that she'd heard the other night.

During the daylight hours the notion that there might be something living up there didn't bother her so much. She'd survived one possum, after all.

During the nighttime, though?

She stepped closer to the fireplace, put her hand on the wimpy wood mantel and listened even harder.

But…nothing.

Her imagination was just getting the better of her. She returned to the kitchen. She drank a glass of tap water and scrolled through her phone messages while she listened to the news on the radio for a few minutes.

But when it morphed into tedious political discord, she turned it off. She also cleared all the missed calls she'd gotten that day.

She didn't recognize any of the numbers and assumed it was reporters from Cheyenne who didn't seem to know when it was time to throw in their collective towel and just leave her alone.

She wiped up the crumbs from her sandwich, flipped the lock on the kitchen door and went into the grooming room. She shut the door after her.

It was getting dark outside so she turned on her lamp, then pulled the sheet she was using as a curtain across the front picture window. If anyone did happen to wander up No Name Road at this point, at least she had privacy inside her impromptu living quarters.

She showered in the dog bath and wondered what was becoming of her when she didn't feel strange about it. Then she tossed the towels over the washing machine—she'd wash them in the morning—and put on a soft gray ankle-length T-shirt.

She returned the air pump to its assigned position on the storage room shelf, plugged her phone in to charge while it played the next chapter in her audio version of *Best Practices for a Successful Dog Grooming Business* and set to work combing the tangles out of her long hair.

When she finally finished the tedious task, she wove the ends into a simple braid and turned off the audio book. She found her app that offered up the soothing sound of ocean waves and collapsed onto her bed.

In the old days, she'd rarely turned in before midnight.

Now, here it was barely nine o'clock and she was dragging.

She reached over and snapped off the lamp, then adjusted her pillows beneath her head and closed her eyes.

Please let me sleep with no dreams tonight.

She'd barely gotten the thought out when her soothing ocean waves turned into a telephone ring. She fell off the air mattress altogether with a hard bump in her scramble to grab her phone.

She peered at the screen but it wasn't Trace's name there.

Just another number she didn't recognize.

She rejected the call and rubbed her hip bone as she rearranged the sheet over herself.

"No dreams," she muttered. "Not about courtrooms. Not about possums or aliens in the chimney." Especially not about Trace.

She tucked the pillow beneath her head and closed her eyes.

The damn phone rang again.

She yanked it close, glared at the number—the same one again—and swiped it. "It's late and if you don't stop bugging me," she greeted coldly, "I'm going to sue you for invasion of privacy and harassment. No matter what my father did, I *do* know my way around the law."

"Ros?"

She bolted upright. "Drake? Is that you?"

"Yeah." His voice sounded unaccountably small and her pulse shot into overdrive.

"What's wrong?"

"We're at the hospital."

She swung her legs off the mattress only to land on her hip bone again. The concrete floor wasn't any softer the second time around. "Are you all right?" She was so rattled she sent the lamp crashing when she reached over to turn it on. "Is your dad okay?"

"He's with the doctor." Drake's voice was thick. He sounded on the edge of tears. "Can you come?"

"Yes." She kept her voice calm even though something inside her chest was squeezing. "The Weaver hospital, right?" Stupid question. There was only one hospital in the entire county. "I'm putting my shoes on right now, so just sit tight. You want me to stay on the phone with you?"

"Mmm-hmm."

She hit the speaker on her phone and turned on the flashlight app since her lamp was in pieces. "I might lose you when I get on the highway but don't worry if I do. I'm still going to get there as quick as I can." She swung the beam of light around until she spotted her tennis shoes. "Are you in the emergency room?" Her mind was bouncing around imagining all the reasons that could have landed them there. From car accidents to horse accidents to heart attacks.

Of course Trace couldn't have a heart attack.

He was only forty!

"Yeah." Drake snuffled audibly. "I've been calling you all afternoon. I tried leaving a message, but it said your mailbox was full. My mom's here and—"

He broke off in heart-wrenching sobs.

"I'm sorry, sweetheart." Her own vision blurred. "Next time, I promise I'll answer my phone no matter what." And she'd deal with the endless messages that had been filling her voicemail for months. She snatched up her purse and a sweater, then threw open the door to the living area.

Translucent eyes reflected the beam of her phone's flashlight in the otherwise dark room and she gasped, falling back while her phone slid out of her nerveless fingers.

Then the eyes disappeared and all she heard were claws.

Scrabbling.

Somewhere.

Drake was saying her name. "Ros?"

She snatched up her phone and raced through the kitchen, practically throwing herself out the door as if the white-eyed *thing* was right on her heels.

"I'm here." She yanked the door closed. "Just, uh, just saw an owl fly past," she improvised because it was better than wondering what sort of beastly thing she'd just locked inside her home.

She fumbled with her key fob as she ran around the building and hit the remote start.

"We used t'have a barn owl." Drake's voice hitched.

If she could just keep them both distracted. "Was it white like Harry Potter's Hedwig?"

"No." He snuffled. "But she had a white face."

"That's kind of cool. Do barn owls always have white faces?"

"I dunno. Maybe it's like people's hair and they have all sorts of colors."

"Suppose there are ginger owls?"

He gave a huff of sound that held at least a fraction of laugh versus sob.

She yanked open her car door and slid inside, throwing her stuff on the passenger seat as she shoved the car into gear. She wheeled around in a tight U-turn and simultaneously fastened her seat belt. "Did the owl actually *live* in your barn?"

"Yeah. And she made a sound like a lady's scream."

"I thought owls hooted."

"Not barn owls. Dad said they're good birds to have 'cause they eat mice and rats and stuff." The Bluetooth suddenly kicked in and Drake's voice came through the car radio, which was very loud in comparison to the speaker on her phone. "She even had babies, too. They flew away, though."

She adjusted the volume. "Baby birds do that." She'd much prefer to find an owl living in her chimney than whatever was actually creeping out at night to attack her in her sleep.

"We had a bat once, too. They eat lots of bugs." He was clearly warming to his subject.

Which was the goal, she reminded herself, even if the idea of a bat was horrifying in itself. Her headlights swept over the empty road and she hit the gas. "I still wouldn't want one living in my barn." Or my chimney.

"Some bugs are good to have, though. Bees. And praying mantises. Oh, and ladybugs."

"Ladybugs. Right." Insects she could deal with. She careened onto the highway with a squeal of tires and reminded herself that she wasn't going to be any good to Trace and Drake if she landed herself in a ditch. Or worse.

She let up on the gas. There were only a few sets of taillights visible on the road far ahead of her. "My mom used to buy ladybugs to set loose in her garden to keep her plants from getting eaten up by other things." She wasn't sure exactly where that memory came from. "She used to say that a ladybug landing on you was better luck than finding a copper penny."

"Didja ever have one land on you?"

She shook her head even though he couldn't see her. "No, but whenever I found a penny, I always picked it up and stuck it in my piggy bank." She glanced at the Bar-H turnoff when she flew past it. A light shined in the distance, well off from the road. "I had about a hundred of them by the time I was your age."

"That's only a dol—" His voice suddenly cut off and twangy bluegrass music came on.

"Dammit!" She hit the steering wheel with her palm. She'd lost cell service already.

She thumbed a button on her steering wheel, turning off the music.

Just hold on.

She wasn't sure if the prayer in her head was meant more for Drake or for Trace.

Chapter Nine

The emergency entrance of the hospital was lit so brightly Ros saw it long before she turned into the parking lot. She parked near the door, grabbed her sweater and purse and ran inside.

She'd tried calling Drake back once her signal returned but he hadn't answered.

Now, her heart was pounding sickeningly inside her chest.

She stopped at the desk where a young guy with a goatee held a phone to his ear. "I'm looking for Trace Powell and his son, Drake." She held her hand about shoulder-height, not caring that she was interrupting him. "Drake's eight and about this tall. Spiky red hair. His mom is Sherry Powell."

The guy shifted his phone receiver to his other ear and picked up a pen, his gaze lifting to her face. "Who're you?"

Nobody at all.

"Their lawyer," she said with all the authoritativeness she'd ever learned at Martin Pastore's knee.

He pointed with the pen. "Through those doors. Follow the signs to ICU."

She glanced around the waiting area as she headed through the doors. The ICU was cordoned off by another set of double doors. An empty nurse's station with a view of the glass-walled cubicles lining two corridors presented no barrier at all.

She spotted Drake sitting hunched in one of the armless chairs at the very end of the corridor to her left.

She jogged down the hall toward him and swept him up in a hug when he launched himself at her.

"It's okay," she soothed, even though she wasn't in any position to be certain of anything. She had to swallow past the knot in her throat. "Was it an accident? Where's your mom?"

Drake nodded and jabbed his thumb toward the room next to the chairs. The curtain inside had been pulled all the way across the glass wall. "My dad's in there with her." His freckles stood out against his pallor and tears turned his eyes to emerald green. "Doctor Morgan said I gotta wait out here 'cause it's the rule."

"How long ago was that?"

"I dunno. Ten minutes maybe." He kicked over one of the empty water bottles sitting on the floor next to the chairs. "I think they should let kids see their moms and dads when they want."

She tended to agree.

She tossed her purse and sweater on the empty chair next to his and gently brushed his hair back from his sunburned forehead. He seriously needed to learn to use sunblock. Then she was annoyed at herself for even having that thought right now. “Have you had anything besides water? Something to eat?” Surely his mother would have made sure of that, too.

He lifted one shoulder and shifted from one foot to the other. “We went to the cafeteria for supper but I wasn’t very hungry.”

She took his hands in hers again. “Do you want me to sit here with you or see what I can find out?”

“See what you can find out.”

She forced a smile and leaned over to brush a kiss on his head. Then she walked over to the cubicle, smoothing her still-damp hair back from her face.

Her heart was thumping hard as she reached for the edge of the sliding door. It felt heavy as she pushed it open enough to slip through and grab the edge of the curtain.

Sure, she had no authority besides an eight-year-old’s to be there but just let anyone try to kick her out.

She pulled in a quick breath, and boldly stepped around the edge of the curtain, bracing herself to meet Trace’s ex-wife.

But when her gaze hit the hospital bed dominating the center of the room, fresh dread swamped her as she took in the beeping monitors. The tubes and cords. And the bandages.

They swathed nearly every inch of the patient on the bed. And what wasn’t bandaged looked bruised and battered.

She felt a hand on her arm and her breath hitched.

She turned and looked up at Trace, who leaned against the wall by the door, looking haggard.

She didn't know what propelled her. But she could no more stop herself from wrapping her arms around his neck than she could stop her heart from thundering inside her ears. "I thought you were the one who was hurt," she whispered thickly. And after that point, she realized she hadn't thought logically at all.

His fingers grazed her back. Her waist. "It's Sherry," he said under his breath.

But Ros had already figured that out.

She looked toward the bed again. At the flaming red hair peeking from beneath the gauze wrapped around his ex-wife's head. Below the gauze, her face was covered in purple bruises.

A tall blonde nurse in blue scrubs stood alongside the hospital bed, fussing with the monitors and typing into a computer mounted on a tall, narrow rolling cart while a shorter woman in a white coat leaned over the patient with a stethoscope in her hand.

Ros realized she was still clinging to Trace and let go. "Did you know Drake called me?"

"Yeah. He called while I was signing some paperwork at the nurse's station. He didn't tell me you were coming, though."

She was intruding. "I'll go back out and sit with him. Has he seen his mom yet?"

Trace's broad shoulders moved restlessly. "Not since they took her back for surgery. The surgeon's supposed to be coming to fill me in, but—" He broke off when the shorter woman turned toward him. "This is Dr. Morgan," he introduced.

"The anesthesiologist," the unsmiling woman added. "Despite appearances, everything is looking good so far." She pocketed her stethoscope and left.

"They're keeping her in a coma," Trace said after the doctor was gone. He rubbed his hand over his eyes and down his dark beard.

"Hang the rules," Ros whispered. "Drake should come in and see her."

He nodded. "I know."

"I agree." The nurse turned on silent shoes toward them. Her nametag said "Courtney" and her expression was much warmer than Dr. Morgan's. "But only for a few minutes. Then if you want to go to the family waiting room, I'll come and find you when Dr. Gupta is ready to talk with you. There are more comfortable chairs there. A television. Vending machines and such."

"Where is it?" Ros asked.

"Sccond floor. You won't be able to miss it when you get off the elevator. Meanwhile, I'll check on Dr. Gupta." She pulled the curtain partially aside before wheeling her computer cart through the doorway.

Drake stood on the other side of the glass. His eyes were saucers and fresh tears slid down his cheeks.

Ros blinked hard and stepped out of Trace's way so he could go to his son.

He went on his knee and Drake buried his head on his father's shoulder.

Trace's fingers spread over Drake's back as he held him. "I know you're scared, son. But your mom's going to be okay. We talked about this earlier, right?"

Drake nodded. His voice was muffled against Trace's shoulder. "The stronger I believe it, the more she'll feel it. But what if—"

"No what-ifs," Trace said. Not quite sternly. Not quite comfortingly. He pushed Drake away by the arms. "Look me in the eye."

Drake swiped his face again. Finally lifted his chin and looked at his father.

"You trust me?"

Drake nodded.

"I know she looks bad right now, but she's always been a fighter. She loves you more than anything, and right now underneath all those bandages and bruises she's fighting harder than she's ever fought before. Just so she can get back to you. So you got a duty to fight right along with her. That means you gotta believe, Drake. Harder than you ever thought you could believe. And she'll know."

Ros looked away and dashed the tears from her eyes.

"Can I go in and see her?"

Trace nodded. His gaze found Ros's as he straightened.

They both watched Drake slip into the room and

go to the side of the hospital bed. He sent a look over his shoulder at them and Trace nodded again. “Go ahead,” he said quietly.

Drake slowly touched his mom’s fingers where they lay curled against the sheet. Then he slid his hand underneath them and rested his head on the top of the rail surrounding the bed.

Ros folded her arms around herself, pressing a fist against the ache in her chest. “I should leave the two of you—”

“No.” Trace’s hand closed over her shoulder. “Don’t go.”

She looked up at him. But his eyes were focused on his son and ex-wife through the glass partition.

She told herself she gave in for Drake’s sake.

The boy stayed in the room for several minutes until Courtney returned again. “Dr. Gupta’s dealing with another emergency,” she told them. “But he wanted me to assure you that the surgery to relieve the pressure on her brain went well and he’ll come up to the family waiting room just as soon as he can.” She gave a comforting smile. “The best thing you can do for Sherry right now is to take care of yourselves, too.”

Trace cleared his throat. When he spoke, his voice was husky. “Thanks, Courtney.”

“We might be a small hospital, Mr. Powell, but we’re mighty.” She smiled gently. “We’re going to take good care of her.”

“Appreciate that.” He cleared his throat again and

waited until she went back to the nurse's station before reentering the cubicle.

Ros watched him put his hand on Drake's shoulder and speak softly. Then the boy lifted his head and, with a lingering look back at his mother, came out of the room with Trace.

Both of them looked shell-shocked. Ros led the way to the elevator and then into the family waiting room.

It was spacious and unoccupied. Trace gestured at the arrangement of chairs and couches. "Wherever you want," he told Drake.

The boy immediately aimed for the couch closest to the flat-screen television mounted on one wall. It was playing an old sitcom.

Trace dropped into a chair not far from him.

And Ros realized how suddenly out of place she felt.

The Powell men didn't need her here. But she also didn't feel right leaving them.

She slipped on her sweater and swung the thin purse strap over her shoulder. "Can I get you a coffee or something?" The vending machines were situated against the far wall, alongside a counter outfitted with a coffeemaker and a microwave.

Trace shook his head. "Get something you want, though."

She didn't want anything. But she felt better being busy, so she went over to the counter and made a production of studying the vending machines and the variety of complimentary pods stacked next to the coffeemaker.

She chose a plain medium roast coffee, stuck the pod in the brewer and hit the button. While the thing gurgled, she wandered over to the windows lining the adjacent wall, pretending to look out. Lamplight illuminated a winding path outside. Mostly, though, she saw the reflection of the waiting room behind her.

Drake was watching the television with glazed eyes.

Trace was sprawled in his chair, tugging on his lower lip.

Her nerves bobbled and she returned to the coffeemaker, waiting for it to finish spitting out the coffee into the disposable cup.

When it was done, she fit the cup into one of the cardboard sleeves stacked neatly on the counter, then went back to the vending machine. She paid for a carton of chocolate milk and a pack of pretzel sticks with a peanut butter dip and set them next to Drake. “They don’t have regular plain milk.”

He offered a polite “thank you” but didn’t reach for either.

She grabbed her coffee and sat down next to Trace. She felt as enthusiastic for her refreshment as Drake did for his, but she sipped it anyway.

Trace was staring at the toe of his boot. “Still can’t believe he called you,” he eventually said.

Ros picked at the edge of her loose-weave sweater.

She wasn't sure how to take that, much less what to say in response.

"Can't believe that you came," he added a moment later.

"Do you really think I would ignore a call like that from Drake?"

His gaze slid to her and ran from her head to her toes, making her acutely aware of her appearance.

Her nightshirt could easily be a dress. There was no way for him to know she was naked underneath.

She still had to fight the urge to pull the lapels of her sweater closed across her breasts.

She shifted in the overstuffed chair and crossed her legs. Her new tennis shoes looked blindingly white.

There was no way to rewind the way she'd hugged Trace at the foot of his ex-wife's hospital bed. No way to take back what she'd said.

But she'd try to ignore it as long as she could.

"Drake said it was an accident?"

Trace nodded. "Semi-truck jackknifed this morning near Rambling Mountain and that new park. What'd they name it? After some old guy who died." He sat forward and rested his elbows on his knees. "Talk about Rambling. *I'm* rambling."

She went still, but he didn't notice because he'd pinched his eyes closed again.

She knew exactly which park he meant. Lambert State Park. Named after Otis Lambert. An old man who'd owned the entire mountain and died without a will.

And her father had been the attorney charged with the duty to impartially administer the estate.

Only there'd been nothing impartial about her father's collusion with Lambert's supposed heir and the mining company waiting in line to buy up every single acre. They'd been very generous in their underhanded deal with Martin Pastore.

It still made her sick. Not only because her father had accepted bribes—which was bad enough on its own—but because she'd believed him when he'd initially blamed it all on Nell.

But Otis Lambert did have a last will and testament, discovered literally at the eleventh hour. His wishes had been honored. The right people had benefited in the end.

Justice had been served.

Because the Lambert matter had turned out to be merely the tip of the iceberg where her father's crimes were concerned.

In a matter of months, Pastore Legal—and everyone who was a part of it, Ros chief among them—came tumbling down.

"Sherry's SUV was the first one in the pileup." Trace's low voice drew her attention back where it belonged.

She chewed the inside of her cheek, studying him. "Does her father know?"

"Seamus and I have no love lost between us, but yeah. I finally got hold of him. He's flying into Cheyenne and renting a car the—" He broke off and stood at the sight of the man in a white coat entering the waiting room.

Ros stood as well and closed her hand around Drake's shoulders when he hurried over, still crunching a pretzel in his mouth. She was relieved he was eating something at least.

Peanut butter once again for the win.

"Mr. Powell?" The surgeon extended his hand. "I'm Dr. Gupta. I apologize for my delay in getting to speak with you regarding your wife."

"Just tell me she's going to recover." Trace's voice was rough. Raw. "That's all I care about."

Ros sucked down her emotions and listened carefully while Dr. Gupta explained the surgery and the possible outcomes.

"The next forty-eight hours will be critical." The surgeon pulled a card from his pocket. "I will be checking on your wife regularly, but this is my service and they can reach me at all times. Call if you have any questions."

"Thank you." Trace pocketed the card. He continued staring at the doorway even after the surgeon had left.

"Are we gonna stay here for forty-eight hours?" Drake asked, which seemed to snap Trace out of it.

"No. *You're* not." He glanced at Ros. "Can you—"

"Anything you need."

There was no doubting the relief in his eyes, which helped make the ache inside her chest bearable.

He looked at Drake. "Ros is going to take you

home now. She'll stay with you at our place." He shot her a quick, questioning look and she nodded again.

"But I don't wanna leave you," Drake protested.

"I get it, buddy. But it's after midnight. Your mom would have a fit if she knew you were up this late. I need you to do this for me, Drake. Okay?"

Drake finally nodded. "Yessir."

Trace cupped his big hand around Drake's head and leaned over, kissing it. "Good man," he murmured.

Then he straightened and looked at Ros. "Let me know when you get there, would you?"

"The minute we're in the door," she promised. "What about you? What do you need?"

"For this nightmare to be over."

She was torn apart by her feelings. She didn't want to leave him alone here at the hospital. But it was obvious to her that his heart was still with the woman in the hospital bed.

"Take some of your own advice, gunny," she told him quietly. "Believe. Harder than you ever thought you could. And she'll know."

Chapter Ten

Sunlight was creeping above the edges of the horizon when Trace stepped quietly through the side door of his house the next morning.

He didn't bother turning on a light once he was inside, and still managed to drop his hat unerringly on the peg as he passed it on his way through to the kitchen.

He stopped and frowned.

The light over the stove—the one that neither he nor Drake ever turned on—was lit. It cast a small welcoming glow in the otherwise dark room.

Had Ros left it on for her own benefit?

Or his?

He shook his head, as if to eliminate the inane thought. "It's just a damn light."

He opened the refrigerator door, grabbed the jug of milk and drank straight from it.

Milk. Macho comfort drink.

He put the cap back on and stuck the container back in the refrigerator before heading through the house. When he reached the top of the stairs, he quietly turned in the dark and entered Drake's room.

The window blinds weren't quite closed and faint light crept through the slats making it easy for Trace to see his son, sprawled on his back.

He had one leg hanging off his twin-size bed the way he always did whenever he was overtired. Trace didn't chance waking him by attempting to unwind the sheet tangled around Drake's ankle. He turned instead to the other twin bed to grab the extra blanket.

And realized just in time that the bed was occupied by Ros.

She was on her side, her back toward him. One hand was curled beneath her head and the pillow, the other rested on her cell phone next to her. Her long braid hung off the side of the mattress.

He reached out and slowly drew the edge of the blanket up and over her hip. His fingertips barely touched her, but he still felt her warmth.

She made a soft sound and rolled onto her back. She stretched her arm over her head and the fabric of her gray dress pulled tight over her breasts.

His fingers curled against his palm.

Keep it moving, gunny.

He retreated to his bedroom and closed the door behind him.

No woman had slept under his roof since he'd come back home to stay.

Hell of a note that she was doing it on the spare bed in his son's bedroom.

He scrubbed his hands down his face. Felt the beard. He'd had one since he left the service.

I don't like beards.

He suddenly chuckled soundlessly.

Then he kicked off his boots and fell facedown on his bed.

He'd shave when he woke up.

Maybe.

"You just tap it on the edge of the bowl. Only not superhard or you're gonna get shells."

Trace could hear Drake's voice as he crossed to the kitchen.

He'd slept longer than he'd intended. Nearly three hours.

Six years of civilian life and he'd gotten as lazy as Purdy Boy.

"What happens if I get shells?" he heard Ros ask.

"Pick them out. Nobody likes shells in their scrambled eggs. Or I guess you could start over."

"We only have five eggs. I don't think we can afford starting over."

"Then don't get shells," Drake said reasonably.

Trace peered around the corner into the kitchen.

Drake was perched on a bar stool, hunched over an ancient stoneware bowl on the island counter between him and Ros. A carton of eggs lay open beside the bowl. Ros had one egg in her hand as if she were weighing it. Or weighing her options for how best to break it.

Morning sunlight was shining through the windows right on her. She'd taken the braid out and her hair flowed over one shoulder in a mass of raven ripples. She didn't have a lick of makeup on her face and he realized she hadn't the night before at the hospital, either. She did, however, still have a bandage on the finger with the splinter.

"Maybe you should do it," she told Drake.

"Jeez, Ros. It's only an egg."

"I'm aware." She tapped it so gingerly against the bowl that it didn't even make a sound.

"Harder than that. It's gotta *crack*, you know."

Trace smiled.

"Smarty-pants." She glanced up then and saw Trace.

This time the cracking sound was more than noticeable.

She'd split the shell right in two, and the egg was running down the outside of the bowl. "You're awake," she said faintly. "How's your—how's Sherry?"

He walked into the kitchen. "The same." He'd already verified that with the hospital.

Drake frowned and Trace rubbed his head, making the hair look even wilder. "She's not worse," he said. "And that's a good thing." He rounded the island and stopped next to Ros. "Now, what have we got going on here?"

Drake folded his arms and leaned on the wood counter. "Didja know that Ros never made scrambled eggs in her whole *life*?"

"I do now." He was perfectly aware of the way she tried sidling away from him, but she could only go so far since she was basically stuck between him and the sink. "How *do* you get through life without making scrambled eggs?"

She raised her eyebrows. "Perfectly well actually, thanks to microwaveable everything, takeout and enormous jars of peanut butter." She turned her back on him to rinse her sticky fingers under the faucet.

Drake grinned at Trace.

He grinned back.

"I noticed your truck outside when we woke up this morning," she said above the running water. "I never heard you come in, though."

"Stealth is my specialty." He plucked out the half of the eggshell that had fallen into the bowl and reached around her to toss it in the sink.

She turned off the faucet and snatched the towel that he handed her. She sent him a sideways look. "You trimmed your beard."

He rubbed his cheek. If he'd gone any shorter, it would be stubble. What he'd considered at the crack of dawn and what he'd considered while eyeing his mug in the mirror ten minutes ago were two different things.

He wished he'd done nothing because now she'd think he'd done it for her.

He had.

But looking into her brilliant blues, he felt about as smooth as a greenhorn.

At least his beard grew fast. It'd be back to normal in a week, tops.

"Is my mom gonna wake up soon?"

Ros raised an eyebrow at him when he hesitated. As he reached around her, his arm just happened to press against hers.

He finally moved aside and looked at Drake. He was wearing a Saint Patrick's Day T-shirt. It was only four months old and already a size too small. "Hopefully very soon, buddy."

He grabbed a paper towel to wipe up the rest of the egg mess that was oozing toward the edge of the counter. "Your grandpa got in. He was sitting with your mom, so I came home to catch some shut-eye and get the chores done."

"We can go see her, though, right?"

He nodded. "But later."

"After chores."

"I was thinking about breakfast first." He threw away the paper towel, then moved around to Drake's side of the island and folded his arms on the counter, too. He smiled at Ros. "Gotta crack some eggs to make an omelet," he prompted while she just stood there twisting his mom's ancient towel to death.

She tossed it aside and plucked another egg from the carton. "Nobody said anything about an omelet. And I never needed to make scrambled eggs myself because someone else always did it."

"Your mom, you mean?" Drake asked.

She shook her head. "I didn't live with my mother. I lived with my father. And he always had a cook."

Drake scrunched his face. "Like at a restaurant?"

"Only in our own home," she said with a nod.

"Dude," Drake marveled. "Were you rich?"

"Not in a way that mattered." Looking determined, she tapped the egg twice on the stoneware edge, then split it open and the contents poured neatly inside the bowl.

She smiled and leaned over, slapping her palm against Drake's.

Trace looked away from the gentle, seductive sway of her breasts and went back around the island to get the jug of milk from the fridge.

It had been nearly full when he'd taken his crack at it this morning. Now, it was almost empty.

He looked over his shoulder at Drake. "You drink all of this already?"

Drake nodded.

"Gonna need a dairy cow to keep up with you." He drank the last remaining mouthful and dropped the bottle in the sink. Then, because he was apparently now a masochist, he stood behind Ros, close enough to look over her shoulder. "Go any slower with those eggs there and we'll be having 'em for lunch."

"Would you like to do this?" She gave him a cool stare. Tiny starbursts of white and yellow radiated from her pupils.

Maybe that's why they always looked so vividly bright.

"And cheat you out of this educational opportunity?" He retreated around the island again.

"We should get chickens, too," Drake said. "Then we could grow our own eggs like Sammy Lee."

"Maybe growing eggs is part of her soccer success," Ros suggested.

Ever since soccer season had started, Trace had heard a lot about Sammy Lee. "Her equivalent of Popeye's spinach?"

"I don't like spinach," Drake said. "If we got a dairy cow, would I get t'milk her?"

Trace chuckled. "Don't take everything so literally. We're not getting a dairy cow." He dragged his finger along the edge of skin showing beneath Drake's too-short shirt and his son wriggled away, giggling.

Meanwhile, Ros cracked another egg and deposited the shell in the egg carton.

"So your mom and dad were divorced just like mine, huh?"

Ros didn't look up from the tiny splinter of shell left floating in the raw eggs that she was trying to capture with her finger. "They were divorced," she answered. "But not like your mom and dad."

"Try touching it with a larger piece of shell," Trace suggested. "It's like a magnet. Shell draws to shell." He handed her one of the pieces from the egg carton.

She looked skeptical but slid the half shell out of his fingers and dabbed it into the bowl. When it came away with the shard stuck to it, she stared as if she'd just seen sliced bread for the first time. "Well, that's too easy."

"They weren't like my mom and dad how?" Drake persisted.

Her gaze skittered over Trace before she focused on the eggs again.

Two to go. She picked one up and cradled it in her palm. "They didn't get along," she told Drake. "At all. Once they're cracked, aren't I supposed to mix in some milk or something?"

"Grandpa mixes in *mayonnaise*," Drake said. "Says it makes 'em supercreamy."

"So does cooking 'em low and slow," Trace countered. "Which is a good thing, because we're out of milk," he said pointedly, "and mayonnaise ain't going into scrambled eggs under this roof. Not while I'm alive to say something about it." He went around the island again, grabbed a small frying pan from the cabinet and set it on the stove. "Time's wasting, Rosalind."

She sent him a look, but at least it didn't contain the solemnness that was there when she talked about her mom and dad.

She cracked the two remaining eggs in succession and stirred them with a fork while he plopped a chunk of butter into the pan and waited for it to melt.

"Can we have bacon, too?"

Ros looked a little harried. "Bacon? Why not toast? I'm an expert at toast."

"Cheater bacon," Trace said. He pulled the package from the fridge. "Already cooked. Heat it up and we're good to go."

"My mom only likes turkey bacon," Drake said. He stuck his tongue out like he was gagging. Then he propped his chin on his hand and sighed heavily. "I bet she'd like some when she wakes up, huh."

Ros leaned over and squeezed his face between her palms. "What she's going to like most is seeing this face." She straightened again.

"She's right." Trace slid the package of bacon across the island, followed by the roll of paper towels and a paper plate. "Open that up. You know the drill."

Drake peeled open the package and layered the bacon slices and paper towels on the plate. Then he got up and stuck it the microwave and bounced on his toes as he watched the timer begin ticking down.

The kitchen wasn't exactly small. When Trace inherited the place, he'd put a little money into it. Modernized a few things. Which just meant that the kitchen had fewer walls, newer appliances and an island counter big enough to accommodate a few people around it. But with the three of them all standing in the work area together, the space was cozy.

The last time man, woman and child had been in

this kitchen together at the same time, it had been him with his mom and dad.

"Is the butter burning?"

Trace jerked the pan off the burner. He looked over Drake's head at Ros. "Let's have those eggs."

She handed him the bowl and he tipped them into the sizzling butter, adjusting the flame to the lowest possible level without extinguishing it. Then he set the pan back on the grate.

"Don't go beating 'em with this." He handed her a wooden spoon that was probably older than the tea towel and nudged her into place in front of the stove. "Just push them around a little as they start to thicken up and set."

"This would be easier if you'd just do it."

He closed his hand around hers and directed the spoon she waved in his face back to the pan. "But would it be this much fun?"

She looked up at him. They were so close he could have kissed her if he lowered his head. Her lips parted slightly and he saw the rise of her breasts as she drew in a long, slow breath.

The microwave dinged loudly.

"Bacon's done," Drake announced needlessly.

Trace cleared his throat and dragged his eyes away from her.

Bacon wasn't the only thing that was done.

"Five eggs don't go very far," Ros observed not even ten minutes later while she savored the last piece of bacon. She'd only gotten it because Trace swatted Drake's hand away from the plate.

The three of them were sitting on the bar stools around the island.

Ros on one side.

Trace safely on the other side with Drake.

"Not with hungry men around." Trace bumped Drake's shoulder and pointed at the sink. "Rinse your plate and get some boots on your feet and I'll let you drive the UTV down to the mailbox to see if the newspaper came."

Drake dashed the plate beneath the water and shoved it in the dishwasher with a clatter before running out of the room.

"And find one of your hats," Trace yelled after him.

"I will." They heard Drake's feet pounding across the great room floor and then up the stairs.

For a guy who'd once managed the logistics of herding an entire company of marines, he'd planned that horribly.

Because now, he and Ros were alone.

She slid off her bar stool, rinsed her plate and fit it into the dishwasher much more quietly than Drake had. Then she turned her back to the sink. "I should be going."

Yet she didn't seem to be making any effort to move away from the sink. Instead, she rested her hands on the counter at her sides.

Trace swung his leg over the bar stool and walked toward her, not stopping until they were toe to toe.

Her eyes widened slightly but she didn't look away.

Then he picked up her hand and whipped the adhesive bandage off her fingertip. "I knew it."

She tugged. "It's fine."

He carefully felt the swollen, red tip. "You saying that doesn't hurt?" He pulled out his pocketknife.

She made a face, yanking on her hand. "Not that much."

But he held fast. "Drake is braver than you," he chided softly. "Just hold still." He angled her finger further into the sunlight and deftly flicked the tip of the splinter free so he could pull it out with his fingers. In two seconds, it was done. "Knew a guy once who got gangrene from a splinter." He showed her the long shard before flicking it into the trash. "Had his arm amputated."

"Are you serious?" She looked appalled.

"No. But he did get a nasty bacterial infection." He spun her around and flipped on the faucet. "Wash."

After she'd done so, he dabbed her fingertip with antibacterial cream and stuck another bandage on it. Then he tossed the tube and box of adhesive strips back in the drawer. "Want me to kiss it better?"

Her lashes swept down. "I'm not a child."

He slipped his hands along her jaw and lifted her face. "No, ma'am. You are not."

Then he pressed his mouth softly against hers.

She inhaled on a hiss and her breasts brushed his chest. “That’s not my finger,” she said against his lips.

“No, it surely isn’t,” he agreed, and kissed her again.

Only the knowledge that Drake would be back downstairs at any minute made Trace break the kiss. But the way her lips clung to his had him debating whether he really cared if Drake *did* catch them.

She had better sense.

She pressed her hand lightly against his chest and slipped out from between him and the counter. “I should go,” she said again. “We both have things we need to do.”

He crossed his arms for something to do besides reach for her again. “Thank you,” he said belatedly. “For last night. For all of it.” He followed her into the mudroom.

She pulled on the long blue sweater hanging on the hook reserved for Drake’s backpack, though it was never used for that purpose. “That’s what neighbors are for, isn’t it?” She swept her hair out from beneath the collar.

The simple dismissal jabbed him like a splinter. “I think we’ve left the neighbor stage in the dust, don’t you?”

“Trace.” She pressed her lips together for a moment, then gave him a completely serious look. “Your wife is—”

"Ex-wife," he corrected.

Her eyebrow climbed slightly. "Are you sure about that?"

"Considering the volume of papers involved in the divorce decree, not to mention the amount of money paid to divorce attorneys, yeah. Pretty sure."

"You know what I mean." She wrapped her purse strap over her shoulder, so that the thin strip of leather bisected the valley between her breasts.

His palms itched to cover the hard points of her nipples that stood out beneath the soft gray fabric of her shirt. "Not sure I do."

She clutched the lapels of her sweater. "I saw your face last night, Trace. You still have feelings for her. An…an emotional connection."

"Yeah. We share a child we both love."

"That's not all she is to you."

"What do you want me to say here, Ros?" Annoyance bubbled inside him. What he wanted was Rosalind. What he didn't want was to hash out his failed marriage. "That if it weren't for Drake she would just be part of my past?" He didn't wait for an answer. "Sherry and I have a history, but that part of it *is* history. We worked damn hard to get to the point where we can just focus on Drake and not on the way we spectacularly failed each other as spouses."

"What are you going to do if—*when*—she needs help after she's well enough to leave the hospital?"

"I'll help her!" He struggled to keep his voice

down. "Doesn't mean I'm still in love with her. If I were, do you think I'd be going around kissing you? Especially when she's lying in a damn hospital bed?"

She shook her head. "This isn't the way divorced people behave."

His aggravation kicked up a notch. "Based on your vast experience, Miz Commitment-Isn't-My-Style? Were you a divorce lawyer?"

Her lips tightened. "No."

"All right, then. Just because your folks didn't get along after they were divorced doesn't mean that's the way for everyone. Not every divorced couple has to be in open warfare all the damn time."

A shutter clanged in place behind her vivid eyes. "There's no reason to have this discussion at all."

"Right. What's a kiss here and there?"

She opened her mouth, but clamped it shut when Drake clattered breathlessly into the mudroom.

"Found my hat," he said, waving it around in the air.

Ros tugged his sleeve. "I've got to go."

Drake's expression fell. "But I thought—"

Trace closed his hands over Drake's shoulders. "Tell Ros thanks for being a good neighbor."

He had to give her credit. The look she gave his son was devoid of the rancor she shot at him.

"She's more than our neighbor." Drake threw his arms around Ros's waist and hugged her tightly. "She's our friend. Right, Ros?"

She didn't look at Trace as she hugged the boy

back. "Of course I'm *your* friend," she assured him before pulling open the door.

Trace watched her hair bounce around her shoulders as she marched toward her car.

How had everything gone so wrong so fast?

Chapter Eleven

"Did you know you have some skinny guy up on your roof?"

"Nell!" Ros looked up from the ledgers spread across the kitchen table. It was no longer serving as her outdoor workbench but as a possible reception desk near the front door of Poocheez.

A front door that was, hallelujah of hallelujahs, finally functional and sporting a brand-new lock.

She went over to hug her and the baby. "Actually, I do know there's a skinny guy on my roof. Why didn't you tell me you were coming?"

"Because I didn't know I was until I decided to drive out here." Nell's gaze raced around the room as she carried the baby inside. "But Julia just had another successful appointment with her pediatrician and she wasn't fussing in her car seat so here we are. This place looks *much* better than Ali implied last week." She walked around Ros's table and ledgers, past the cages, grooming table, air mattress and dog bath. She peered through the doorway to the living area. "Why is that room entirely empty while this one is an obstacle course of stuff?"

"That's why Rodney is up there on the roof." Ros held out her arms. "Gimme?"

Nell handed the baby to her and Ros leaned down to inhale Julia's addictively sweet baby scent.

Heavenly.

"Rodney is on the roof…?" Nell prompted.

"Because there are raccoons living in my chimney." She ran her pinkie through Julia's tufts of blond hair, fascinated at the way it was already showing a tendency to curl. It was Archer's color and had Nell's spiral curl. Talk about hitting the jackpot. She finally looked up at Nell, who was watching her with amusement. "What?"

"Sure you're not hearing a ticktock somewhere in your beating chest?"

"Just because I can appreciate a little baby—one that I can give back to her mama, mind you—doesn't mean I'm hearing my biological clock ticking."

"Not exactly what you implied last year when you moved in with Jonathan. You said he wanted a family—"

"I remember what I said." Ros and Nell had lived together more than half their lives by then. Moving in with Jonathan had been a temporary refuge, but right from the start, they'd both known it wouldn't work. "It was an excuse and I shouldn't have said it in the first place."

Within a matter of weeks, Ros had moved out of Jonathan's place again, checked into an extended-stay hotel and buried herself right back into her work.

Miz Commitment-Isn't-My-Style.

She rubbed her cheek against Julia's head. "Turns out the raccoons aren't just the source of the scratching I hear at night, but they're just as responsible for the stink in the living area and the water leak in my shower."

Nell wrinkled her nose and stepped away from the doorway. "Raccoons as in plural? How'd you figure it out?"

"A mama and her rapidly maturing babies, evidently. It's probably not logical, but I was relieved that at least it wasn't a bunch of possums living in there." Even though Rodney had told her possums were less likely to carry rabies than raccoons.

She paced in front of the window, which was shaded from the hot sun by the sheet she now kept there 24/7. The baby was sucking on her fist in the most adorable way. "And I figured it out only because Trace sent Rodney over a few days ago to take a look."

"That was nice of him."

Ros ignored the suggestive lift of Nell's eyebrows.

It had been a week since the accident. A week since Trace had kissed her in his kitchen. A week since he'd said so much as a word to her.

She only knew that Sherry was out of her coma because of Drake. He hadn't been over to help her since the accident, but he called nearly every day.

"Rodney owes Trace a favor. So..." She shrugged as if she weren't still feeling consternated over the entire matter. Rodney had told her who sent him when he'd shown up on her doorstep out of the blue the other day. She didn't like feeling beholden to Trace, but now she owed him. Because Rodney had absolutely refused her efforts to pay him for his services.

"He trapped the animals yesterday and relocated them, I don't know. Somewhere. He's been cleaning the chimney today and fixing it so they won't try moving back in. Evidently chimneys and raccoons are a match made in heaven."

"Until someone lights a match to burn a fire in the fireplace."

They shared a grimace and Ros picked up a stack of flyers sealed in plastic wrap. "What d'you think?"

Nell peered through the clear wrap. "Grand opening. Buy one service, get one free. Nice way to bring people in the door."

"Let's hope. I mean, this *is* the only dog-grooming service around. So." She couldn't allow herself to think about all the reasons she could fail.

"And you decided to keep Poocheez as the name, I see. Did you get these done in Braden?"

"Online. Less expensive." Ros tossed the brick of flyers on the table and turned her attention back to Julia. "I think she's grown already."

"She has." Nell stroked her baby's head. "We received a lot of newborn-size clothes as gifts. They're already too small." She slid a ledger book aside and sat on the edge of the table. "Meredith's birthday party is Saturday."

"So I'm told."

"You're still planning to come, right? Not going to back out?"

Ros eyed her friend. Probably her one true friend in the world. "What'd they do? Con you into being the one to ask me?"

Nell didn't flinch. "Can you blame them?"

She pressed her cheek against the top of the baby's head again and closed her eyes. "Ali told me Meredith never wanted birthday parties before because I wouldn't come." She exhaled. "You know, it stinks to high heaven that I get that dumped on me. I'm *always* the bad guy."

"No, your dad was always the bad guy and you just didn't know it."

"It's too early for wine, I suppose."

Nell smiled slightly. "Two in the afternoon. I'm going to say yes, it's too early."

"I have iced tea." Ros led the way to the kitchen. She surrendered the baby to Nell and filled two glasses, tore off a few paper towels from the roll and carried everything out back.

Nell took in the arrangement of padded all-weather furniture and the table with its jaunty striped umbrella protruding from the center. "Nice setup."

"You ought to know. Archer's the one who delivered it." And it was ridiculous that every time she sat in one of the chairs, she wished she had the ancient webbed lawn chairs back.

Nell smiled slightly and arranged Julia on her lap. The baby swung her arms and kicked her feet jerkily. "That's your daddy," she cooed. "Doing those annoyingly sweet things when you least expect it." She sipped the tea that Ros set on the paper towel in front of her.

Annoying was right. "I don't need anyone's pity," Ros muttered. "Least of all his. I can—"

"Oh, for criminy's sake," Nell said sharply enough to make Julia let out a little wail and Ros stop and stare.

Nell looked peeved. "Nobody pities you. Just because you don't want to think of your own brother and sisters as family doesn't mean any of them feel that way about you. If you only knew—" She huffed and shook her head slightly, then adjusted her blouse and bra and lifted Julia to her breast.

Ros was momentarily distracted. "My God, your boobs are *huge*."

"So my husband routinely points out. He's quite appreciative actually." Nell still looked cross.

Ros waved her hand. "No. Just. No. I don't need to hear about your sex life with Archer."

"Why? Because you're not having any these days? Call up Jonathan again if you're feeling lonely."

She pinched away the vision of Trace hovering behind her eyes.

They'd fallen down a rabbit hole and it was time

to stop. She dropped her hand again. "If I only knew what?"

But Nell grimaced. "It's not my place to say."

"Then why'd you bring *whatever* up at all?" She paced around the table, sipping her tea and feeling restless. "Yes, I'll be at the birthday party. But you can tell Ali I am *not* bringing a date."

Rodney suddenly appeared, wiping his hands on a rag. "All finished up, Miz Pastore." When he saw Nell nursing the baby he went as red as a tomato and looked away at the house as if he were addressing the clapboard siding. "Your chimney's clean as a whistle and you've got a good chimney cap on now. But you keep an eye on it. If you see that cap move or disappear or anything at all, you give me a call." He pulled a business card from his coveralls and extended it toward her, though he was still looking away.

Ros took it and tossed it on the table.

"Raccoons are wily," Rodney warned as he edged his way toward the corner of the building. "They like a spot, they tend to return to it, and they're pretty nimble when it comes to getting past anything standing in their way. So it's real important that you stay on top of it if they decide to come back. Don't want to give 'em a chance to settle back in, you know?"

"I understand, Rodney." She walked with him around the corner of the house. "I appreciate all the work you did."

"Was glad to do it, ma'am. Got me all square with

the gunny again." With a wave, he set off toward his work truck.

She wished his squaring things up with Trace didn't mean that she now had something to square up with the man, too.

She returned to the table and sat down with Nell. "You're my oldest friend. I don't want there to be bad feelings between us."

"I don't, either." Nell rocked slightly in the cushioned seat.

"Then just tell me whatever is sticking in your craw so we can get back to normal."

Nell's expression was serious. "Normal for you used to be worshipping at Martin's feet. Normal was working your tail off at the firm. Not just because it was about the only thing that garnered his approval but because you were *good* at it."

"Not good enough to know what he was up to."

"That's not lack of competence. That was an abundance of trust in the man you thought he was. I just had those particular blinders knocked off earlier than you did. And he wasn't my father."

Ros's throat tightened. No, Nell's real father had simply walked out on her altogether after Nell's mother died.

"Normal—" Nell pointed at the Poocheez sign propped against the wall "—isn't *that*."

"Well, it's what I've got. New normal." Aside from moving it off the kitchen table, Ros hadn't touched the sign since Trace told her she was using the wrong sandpaper. "And you know how much I detest that term. But it's accurate. So? Just spit it out already and let's get on with it."

Nell switched Julia to her other breast, looking as if she was having a silent debate with herself. "Meredith didn't leave your dad because she was having an affair with Carter," she said abruptly.

Of all the things that Ros might have expected, that wasn't it. "Of course she did. She was even pregnant with the triplets. She chose her life—"

"That's your father's narrative," Nell said sharply. "After everything, are you so sure you want to just continue believing it?" She waited a beat. "She left him because he'd been abusive. *Physically* abusive."

Ros leaned back in her chair, not even needing to consider it. "Manipulative and controlling, yes. Conniving? Most definitely." She shook her head. "But he never even raised his voice. At anyone. You know that. He didn't have a temper." He also didn't have ethics, conscience and decency, which she'd never once suspected.

"Ask Meredith," Nell said quietly.

Ros opened her mouth to refuse, but hesitated. Nell had no reason to make up such a thing. And she obviously believed it. A pit started forming in her stomach. "You're serious."

"He branded her with his cigarettes. Yeah. I'm serious." Nell's gaze was steady. "It's not a pretty story."

For Ros's entire life, her mother had been unfailingly cheerful. Unrelentingly positive. It didn't seem possible she'd ever hid anything.

"Nothing's pretty when it comes to Martin Pastore." She pushed out of her chair. "But she obviously told *you* the story." She paced to the kitchen door and then back again. "I suppose *all* of my siblings know, too. Only Ros, who can't handle the truth, is excluded."

"Meredith didn't tell me a single word of it. Archer did. And he only knows because Carter told him. If anything ever happened to Carter, he wanted to ensure that Archer could protect you and Meredith again from Martin. If the need ever arose. He has photographs, Ros. I haven't seen them and I never want to. But Carter gave them to Archer for safekeeping. Just in case."

If Ros didn't know her so well, she'd have accused Nell of emotional manipulation.

But that had been Martin's expertise.

Not Nell's.

Nell clasped Ros's hand. "Meredith's never discussed it with *any* of them. The triplets don't have any idea. It's the past. She wants it kept in the past. She doesn't want her family—especially you—marred by it."

"Too late for that, wouldn't you say? She left me with a man she knew—" Ros pulled away and paced farther toward the graveyard and back again. Her mind was racing. "Don't you see this just proves how little I mattered? Why even tell me?"

"That." Nell pointed a finger at Ros. "That very reason. You don't know how *much* you mattered! How much you have always mattered. This is your history, Ros. Nobody deserves to know the whole truth more than you do. Don't you want to know what that actually is?

"I'll never know why my father left. That question will go unanswered forever. But you can have your answers. All you have to do is talk to Meredith. If not for her sake, then for yours. Then maybe you'll stop feeling like you're an outsider in this family!"

"I'm here!" Ros spread her arms. "I went to the family dinner a few weeks ago. And I said I'd go to her freaking birthday party, didn't I?"

"This isn't about the party. It's about up here." Nell touched her finger to her temple. "And here." She pressed her palm flat against her chest above her nursing baby. "Look. I didn't even intend to bring all this up. But now I have and I can't pretend I'm sorry. If you're going to let Martin's actions rule who you become—"

"Nothing about him rules who I am," Ros countered flatly.

Nell just looked at her for a long moment. "You don't believe that any more than I do," she finally said. "His actions drove you *here*." She sighed. "I love you. You're the sister of my heart. And if you want to be a dog groomer, then be a dog groomer! But don't be one just because you're punishing yourself for having trusted Martin."

"Talking to my mother isn't going to change that."

"It might change the way you feel about her and Carter."

"You want me to have some compassion for a woman who left an abusive man? I do. I applaud her bravery. But you want me to have compassion for a woman who left behind her *child* with that man?"

Nell fastened her blouse and lifted the baby to her shoulder. "We grow up thinking we know how deep the bond is between a mother and her child. We think we know the lengths she will go to for her children. But until I had Julia, I never realized the difference between knowing something and *knowing* something."

"And that's what prompted you to tell me all this now? Because you've got your own perfect little family?"

Nell's eyes searched hers. "I'm one of the last people to champion anything where Martin Pastore is concerned. He's a liar and a thief. But that's not how he raised you. Not every minute was terrible for you growing up as his exalted child. Yeah, he was demanding. But you thrived on the challenge. Always. He never laid a hand on you, did he?"

"Never. But how was *she* to know that? And is it abuse for a parent to put a price on his affection? I had to earn it from him. Had to be the perfect reflection of him. Or what I thought he was. Is this the real reason you came out here? Because Archer just told you about all this?"

"I told you I didn't intend to bring this up! And I've known about this since last year."

Ros stared. "So…what? You kept the secret all this time because I chose to believe my father's lies over you?"

Nell looked pained and pushed out of her chair. "I kept the secret because Archer asked me to. Then I found out I was pregnant. I didn't know if I was going to be disbarred for not immediately reporting what I'd discovered about Martin's actions. Then the federal charges came down against him and…" She sighed, jiggling the baby against her shoulder and patting her back with an unsteady hand. "And you had enough on your plate without adding that, too. But it's bothered me all along that there's this huge element of *your* history that's been kept from you!"

"But you're privy to that history. So why not just finish telling me the whole damn ugly tale and—"

"Because as much as I believe it's your right to know the truth, it's your mother's right to be the one to tell it to you! You've always been a stickler for justice. For truth and fairness. So be fair with yourself. Be fair with your mom!" Nell waved an arm in a gesture encompassing their surroundings. "Look at what you've sacrificed just to make some restitution for what Martin did entirely on his own. Once you and Meredith talk, maybe it won't change how you feel about her or Carter. But maybe it will. Maybe you'll realize that the family you've always wanted has been there all—"

Julia suddenly emitted an entirely undainty burp.

"—along," Nell finished. Then silence fell as she watched Ros warily.

She wrapped her arms tightly around herself and rocked on her heels. "Impressive," she finally said.

"You should hear her when she's had more than just a little snack." Nell dabbed the baby's mouth. "I don't blame you if you're angry with me."

"I'm not angry with you. I'm just—" She groaned. "I don't know what I am."

Nell cocked her head slightly. "Is that a phone I hear—"

"Shoot!" Ros darted past her and inside the building. She snatched her cell phone from where she'd left it beside the ledgers. The number on the display wasn't Drake's or anyone else's she knew but she'd learned her lesson. She answered, anyway. "Yes, hello?"

"Is this Rosalind Pastore?" The female voice was brisk.

She tightened her grip on the phone. "Who's asking?"

"Ms. Pastore, Shonda Simpson again with K-G-W—"

Ros hung up and raked her hair back from her face. She pressed a few more buttons on the phone to block the number. "Reporter," she said when she turned and found Nell there.

"Still?"

She nodded and shoved the phone in her back

pocket. "I don't know why any of them keep trying. There's nothing more to the story."

"Who'd you think was calling? I haven't seen you move that fast since we were teenagers."

She was willing to follow Nell's lead into less fraught waters. "I move fast now." She stuck out a foot and showed off her gleaming white tennis shoe. "I have the appropriate gear, if you'll notice."

"It's never too late to change your phone number."

"That's like letting them win."

Nell raised her eyebrows slightly. Julia was sucking on her tiny fist, looking blissful and drowsy. "You know how ridiculous that sounds, right?"

"I wouldn't change it now, anyway. Drake might call and—" She eyed Nell. "If you make those eyebrows of yours go any higher, they're going to meet on the back side of your head."

"Is this better?" Nell lowered them in a patently false frown. "How *are* things going with your handsome neighbor?"

"Who said anything about Trace?"

"Ali might have mentioned him. I know Drake is his son. But interesting that you knew exactly who I meant."

Ros tossed up her hands. "Hardly an intellectual leap. I only *have* one neighbor."

I think we've left the neighbor stage in the dust, don't you?

She focused blindly on freeing the flyers from the

wrapping. "Drake is the one who calls me. I'm sure Ali told you about him, too."

Nell nodded. "Sounds like a sweet kid."

"He is." She crumpled the plastic in her fist. "But y'all can stop conjuring up scenarios that involve his dad and me. And you can tell Ali I said that, too."

"They're divorced, aren't they? Trace and—"

"Sherry, and yes." She put the wrapping in the trash. "Not that it matters. Regardless of what he told me, it's obvious he's still in love with her."

Nell's gaze followed her as she paced. "I feel like I'm missing something here."

Ros told her about the accident. About Drake calling her and how she'd stayed with him through the night. "I couldn't very well ignore him. He needed me."

Nell was nodding. "Of course. And you spent the night at Trace's place?"

Ros glared. "Don't make it sound like that. It was only because of Drake."

What's a kiss here and there?

"Sure. Sure," Nell said benignly. "Makes sense."

"Exactly. Just because he—" Ros clamped her jaw shut and flipped the ledger books closed. She stacked them on top of each other.

One.

Two.

Nell's eyebrows were climbing again as she waited. *"Yes?"*

"Fine." She slapped the third ledger on top of the

others. “He kissed me. There. Is that what you want to know?”

Nell rested her hip against the table. Her dark eyes were suddenly sparkling. “Did you kiss him back?”

Ros looked at the nonexistent watch on her wrist. “Don’t you have to be getting back to your husband or something?”

“In other words, Why, yes, Nell, my dearest friend, I did kiss him back.”

Ros managed what she hoped was a stony stare.

Nell leaned closer. “How was it?”

“Ordinary. Yet unobjectionable.”

Entirely unobjectionable.

His beard hadn’t been scratchy at all. In fact, it had been soft. Captivating. Like the taste of him. The feel of him. She’d felt herself melting right into him when he’d taken her in his arms.

“That’s an epitaph all right,” came a deep voice from the open front doorway.

Ros’s stomach swooped and she accidentally knocked the stack of ledgers into the flyers. The bright blue-and-white pages literally went flying. “Trace.”

He stepped into the room, picked up one of the flyers from the floor right in front of him and tossed it back on the table.

Her mouth felt dry and her cheeks hot. “Wh-what are you doing here?”

“Hearing what no man wants to hear.” His gaze

skated past her to Nell. And he did that thing he did, flicking the brim of his hat.

It seemed to bemuse Nell as much as it did every other woman, though if he noticed, he didn't show it.

"I brought you something." He pulled two folded lawn chairs into view and propped them against the wall just inside the doorway.

Ros eyed the bright red-and-green webbing that crisscrossed the lightweight metal tubing.

"Still owed you." He tipped his black cowboy hat again, and as abruptly as he'd appeared, he left.

A moment later, she heard the throaty roar of his truck engine and then watched the truck through the doorway as it drove down No Name Road.

Chapter Twelve

Ros heard the raucous music even before the ranch house came into view.

And it grew louder the closer she got.

Pounding drums. Screaming guitars. It made the radio station she listened to on her boom box sound tame.

She parked her car behind Trace's truck and followed the sound toward the long, narrow barn situated beyond the house and the detached garage.

Nell and Julia had left shortly after Trace.

"Talk to Meredith," Nell had urged one last time before she'd driven away with a handful of the flyers that she promised to distribute to everyone she knew.

Ros wasn't ready to decide about Meredith yet. She wasn't sure she'd ever be ready to hear any more details about things that happened a lifetime ago. Things that she couldn't change.

She wasn't really ready to face Trace, either.

It had taken her nearly the rest of the afternoon to get a grip on herself.

He'd sent Rodney.

He'd brought her chairs.

She had to get her act together enough to say a simple thank-you. It was the right thing to do.

The barn door was rolled to one side. Music pulsed like a writhing thing from the shadowy interior.

One "thank you." That's all she needed to offer.

Simple enough.

She took a deep breath, smoothed back her hair and walked into the barn.

She expected to see barn stuff. Bales of hay. Tools. Maybe a tractor.

And she did. She also saw the open door at the opposite end of the barn. And the metal crossbeam in the middle.

But it was the shirtless man, hands hooked over the beam, that quickly became her sole focus and stole every speck of breath in her lungs.

He was facing away from her, doing pull-ups. Shoulders, wide as an ox, flexing. Muscles rippling. Skin gleaming. His training shorts hung loosely from around his hips, which were narrower than she realized. His ankles were crossed. Knees bent. One knee even had a barbell tucked behind it.

She moistened her lips. Pressed her hand against her belly and hunted for air.

How he heard her over the music she would never know.

But he suddenly released the bar and dropped to the hay-strewn floor. He was surprisingly light-footed. Oddly graceful. He caught the barbell before it fell and set it on the floor. Then he propped his hands on his hips. "What do you want, Ros?" he asked even before he turned to face her. His hair fell over his forehead in sweaty spikes.

"You." She nearly choked when she blurted out the word. He'd been hiding all *that* under plain blue cotton shirts? Yes, he was impressive even *in* the cotton. But this—

She was pretty sure her eyeballs were perspiring from the effort it took not to gawk. "I mean, you… you sent Rodney." She had to raise her voice over the raging music.

He picked up a remote sitting on a sawhorse next to a towel and a gallon-size water jug and turned the volume down.

"Raccoons gone?" He snatched the towel and ran it roughly over his face.

"Yes." It was almost a squeak and she was grateful to her soul that his face was buried in white terry cloth, so he'd never see the way she hauled in a quick breath.

Then he ran the towel almost absently down the front of his chest. That wide, gleaming, glorious chest.

She folded her arms and looked down. She scuffed her tennis shoe through the straw sprinkled all around the ground. "You shouldn't have—I mean, I should pay you back. Rodney said he owed you, but—"

"Sixteen-hundred and seventy-two dollars," he said.

Her head came up. "That's what he charges to get rid of raccoons?" She was appalled.

"No idea what he charges for that." He flipped one end of the towel over his shoulder and grabbed the jug of water, tipping it to his lips for a deep, thirsty drink. Then he lowered it to his side and he wiped away a drop of water on his chin with the back of his hand. "But that's what he owed me. I told him to take care of the problem and I'd call it even. You want to pay me back? Sixteen-hundred and—"

"Seventy-two dollars," she finished. "And the lawn chairs—"

"Another thirty-four bucks each." His lips twisted into something that wasn't a smile but wasn't quite a grimace, either. "But we can split that down the middle. Considering."

She cleared her throat. "I, um, I can make payments—"

He swore and shook his head. He capped the gallon jug and balanced it on the sawhorse once more. "You are a piece of work, you know that?"

She jerked up her chin. He might have lowered the music, but she could still hear the bass thumping from the speakers—wherever they were hidden inside the barn. "Why? Rodney isn't the only one who wants to stay square with you."

"Rodney's a twenty-two-year-old kid who needed a course correction in his life. I could bail his ass outta jail and help him find the straight and narrow on his own, or walk him down to the recruiter's office for four years of a life that would kill his mama since she'd already lost Rodney's brother." Trace's voice was even. “You need—” He propped his hands on his hips and shook his head. “Hell. I don’t know what you need.”

Her gaze roved over the smattering of dark hair blooming across his chest. She could think of one thing in particular that she needed. Badly.

Realizing she was gawking, after all, she yanked her thoughts out of the bedroom. Not to mention the pile of straw over in the corner. Or any other readily available surface.

She hugged her arms tighter across her chest. Her breasts felt so tight they ached and there was a hollowness deep inside her that defied description. All for a man who was hung up on his ex-wife.

“Where’s Drake?”

“With Seamus at the hospital.”

She chewed the inside of her lip. Her eight-year-old chaperon wouldn’t come to the rescue, then.

“Any other questions? Anything else you want to toss back in my face?”

“I don’t know why you’re so peeved.” She felt the irritation rising in her nervous system, exacerbated by every other part of her disturbing afternoon. “All I’m trying to do is start fresh. Without owing anyone anything. What’s wrong with that?”

“Not a damn thing.” His voice was flat. “In fact, it’s perfectly ordinary.”

She didn’t know why it took her so long.

Maybe because she was having her first-ever

honest-to-goodness struggle with sheer, unadulterated lust.

But the speed at which irritation turned to fury made her feel dizzy.

"You big, emotional—" she crossed toward him in three long strides, and jammed her finger hard against his chest "—lummox!" Now her finger ached, because it was like jamming her finger against a solid brick wall. "You think I was saying that kissing you was...*blah*?" She jabbed him again.

Which was a dumb move because it only hurt more.

He grabbed her finger before she could poke him again. "What was it, then?"

"*Ex*traordinary," she said through her teeth. And she wanted to kick him for making her say it. "Kissing you—" Her throat tightened.

She realized he was sliding his palm against hers. Slipping his fingers through hers.

"K-kissing you," she tried again. "Was...felt like—"

He dragged her an inch closer. "Like?"

Her eyes burned deep inside her head. *Coming home.* The words reverberated through her chest and her breath hitched. "It felt right," she managed, which was true, too, but so much less than the whole truth. "The way it's supposed to feel."

He sank his free hand through her hair, tilting her head back. His mouth found hers.

It hadn't been a fluke, that first time.

Warmth spread out from her lips. Coursed through

her head. Her body. Her heart. Even her hair felt on fire from him. “Trace—”

“Shh.” He angled her head and deepened the kiss. He released her hand but only to grab her around the waist and lift her against him, pulling her thighs around his hips.

Her head swam. Her fingers sank through his hair. His beard was soft. Rough. His mouth was hot. Tender.

Then she felt something behind her. The sawhorse, she realized, and he was leaning against her, pulling her even tighter. Closer.

She twined her legs around him. Sank her hands inside the waistband of his shorts and felt the smooth, hard curve of naked rear and—

He suddenly swore and jerked back, looking down between them at the water that was pouring out of the gallon-jug all over her legs.

She pressed her forehead against his throat and laughed breathlessly. “Almost better than a shower in the dog bath.”

He clasped her face, turning it up to his again. “Honey, I don’t know what the hell that’s supposed to mean. But if you want to stop, say so now, because—”

She pressed her fingers to his lips and looked into his muddy green eyes. “I’m not saying stop,” she whispered. She’d worry about later…later.

His pupils dilated. “Hold on.”

She wrapped her arms around his wide shoulders and linked her calves around his waist. He picked her up and carried her toward the far door of the barn, but before he reached it, he turned into a room she hadn't even noticed and followed her down onto an ancient leather couch wedged against one wall.

His office, she thought dimly as his hands delved beneath her wet jeans.

And then she didn't think anymore.

She just opened everything that she was to his touch.

The sun was just beginning to dip toward the horizon when they finally moved again.

"Come on." Trace pushed up from where he'd been sprawled buck-naked on the floor next to the couch. He held out his hand, and once he'd pulled her to her feet, he led her out of the office again.

She was still so numb from pleasure her brain was firing two seconds too slowly. "Wait. My clothes—"

"Don't need 'em. Or are you too refined to go naked when there's nobody around for miles?" He tugged her out the barn door.

"Refined doesn't have anything to do with bare feet." She danced around on her toes as they reached gravel. "My shoes—"

"You are a trial, you know that?" But he was grinning as he said it and he just lifted her off her feet again.

Before she could swoon too much over the romantic gesture, though, the world tipped as he tossed her unceremoniously over his shoulder.

"Hey." She smacked his butt. It really was a phenomenal butt. Almost as unyielding as his chest and almost close enough to sink her teeth into if a woman felt so compelled. "What do you think you're doing?"

"Saving your feet." He clamped his arm over her thighs and walked, bold as brass, across the gravel toward the house.

His bare feet had to be as cast iron as the rest of him.

If she'd thought he would put her down, though, once they reached the house, she was mistaken.

Her head bounced against his back as she stared at the cowboy boots arranged messily around the wood-plank bench in the mudroom. She tried to keep her head lifted as he carried her through the kitchen.

A coffee cup sat on the butcher-block island.

She finally lowered her cheek against his spine after he crossed the great room and reached the staircase. Her heart was thudding again. "You *could* put me down any time now. I do have two perfectly operable legs."

She felt his beard against her hip. Then a kiss that set off an entirely fresh conflagration.

"I'm very aware," he said.

When he started up the stairs, she wrapped her arms around his waist to keep from bouncing so much. "Being upside down like this, it would serve you right if I got carsick."

There was no possible way she could tell that he was smiling. Not from her...perspective.

But she still knew.

He reached the top of the stairs and finally turned into a room where he flipped her down onto a wide bed covered with a faded patchwork quilt.

His eyes stared into hers. "Feeling sick?"

She shook her head and eyed him as boldly as he was eyeing her. It was so much easier to do that than to dwell on the trembling inside that went clear to the very heart of her. She didn't do relationships. Didn't fall in love.

Especially with someone she had only known for a matter of weeks.

Then why does he feel like home to you?

She swallowed the notion. "For an old guy you're pretty—"

"I'll give you old." His teeth flashed as he wrapped his hands around her ankles and kissed one. Then the other.

She gasped. "Just telling you what your son thinks."

"Much as I love my kid—" he'd reached her inner knee "—I'm not thinking about him right at the moment." He watched her as he slowly made his way upward. Inward.

She nearly shot off the bed when his mouth found her. Then he was moving again, his mouth burning up her belly to her breasts. Stopping to linger where her pulse thundered beneath her ear. Now she was nearly begging him.

Only then did he thread his fingers through hers and slowly, inexorably, fill her.

"That feel old?" His voice was deep and hoarse against her ear.

She shook her head, blindly seeking his mouth with hers. "Don't stop."

And he didn't.

Not even when helpless, inexplicable tears began leaking from the corners of her eyes.

He just softly kissed them away, sneaking even further into her heart as he gathered her ever closer.

And together, they flew.

She was a pillow hog.

Trace rested his head on his hand and watched Ros sleep while he idly combed his fingers through her silky hair.

Dark skeins of it streamed across her pillow. And his pillow.

Because she'd wrapped her arm around both, stealing his right out from under his head.

He might not feel old when it came to the woman in his bed, but she'd whipped every lick of strength he had right out of him all the same.

If he closed his eyes, he'd sleep, too.

Which he didn't want to do, because Seamus would be dropping Drake off any time now.

What he needed to do was get his rear out of bed and downstairs.

He still lay there another five minutes.

Then five more on top of that.

Just because watching Ros Pastore sleep was that sweet a sight.

But finally, he made himself move.

It was nearly seven.

He rooted through the bedding that had landed on the floor and untangled the sheet so he could flip it lightly over her long limbs. Then he grabbed clean clothes. Rather than using his own attached bathroom and risk waking her, he went down the hall to Drake's.

He was showered and dressed and heading downstairs just in time to hear his son bursting through the kitchen door.

"Dad," he yelled. "I'm home." Trace heard the thump of boots and backpack hitting the floor.

He rounded the wall to the kitchen and stopped dead at the sight of Seamus following Drake in from the mudroom.

Up to now, Seamus had contented himself with dropping off Drake at the door before heading on to Sherry's apartment where he'd been staying. Trace could be civil to the man for his son's sake. Even for Sherry's sake. But that didn't mean it was easy.

He moved his coffee cup from that morning to the sink and leaned against the counter, his arms crossed over his chest. "Seamus," he greeted in an even tone.

"Powell."

"Mom's getting released from the hospital," Drake announced. Drake's smile was broad, in contrast to the perpetual scowl on Seamus's face.

Trace couldn't help a jerk of surprise. "Already?" He looked at Seamus.

"Her doc's thinking by the end of the week. Beginning of next for sure."

That sounded more like it.

"She's gonna have a walker," Drake said. "So she doesn't fall. But she's gotta get better using it, too. And she's not s'posed to try going up or down stairs at all." He yanked open the fridge, pulled out a carton of milk and started to lift it straight to his mouth.

Then his eyes widened as his gaze went past Trace.

He didn't need to turn around to see Ros. Not when his nerves prickled every time she came within shouting distance.

But he did sneak a look just to be sure she hadn't come down the stairs as naked as they'd gone up them.

Pillow hog.

And now, fortunately, closet raider.

She wore one of his oldest denim shirts. The shirttails reached nearly to her knees. With the sleeves rolled up and—he had to look twice—one of his leather belts tied like some kind of sash around her waist, she made the thing look like a stylish dress.

She'd brushed her hair and it hung in a shining curtain over one shoulder. The smile on her face when Drake launched himself at her made something tighten inside Trace's chest.

"Ros!" Drake looked as if he were trying to

squeeze the stuffing out of her. Either that or lift her right off her feet. "My mom's getting outta the hospital soon."

She smiled brilliantly into Drake's face. "That's the best news." With her arm still wrapped around him, she looked toward Seamus. "Is this your grandfather?"

Drake nodded. "Grandpa. This is our friend Ros."

Ros's blue eyes skimmed over Trace's face before she focused again on Seamus.

He had to give her props. She stretched her hand out toward Seamus as if she were genuinely pleased to meet him. "Mr. Shaw. Rosalind Pastore. You must be very relieved about your daughter."

Trace knew how firm her handshake was. No limp-fish offering of fingertips.

And Seamus was surprised by it, too. That, and the fact that Ros didn't shy away from the matter of Sherry.

Trace figured that was more for Drake's benefit than Seamus's.

"I am," Seamus muttered. The tips of his ears were red. "I… I've been meaning to call you back, Miss Pastore. A-about Poocheez."

"Ros," she suggested, sounding warm, though her blue eyes were sharp as lasers.

"I, uh, well, I hope you're settling in there all right."

"I'll admit, I expected the condition to be more in line with your claim that the living quarters were actually habitable." She waited a beat. "But I am managing, thank you."

The red spread from Seamus's ears to his face and throat. "Ah—"

Her smile was so beautiful it was deadly. "It's fortunate that the grooming salon is quite adequate. Otherwise we would be having a much different conversation."

If Trace didn't enjoy seeing that deadly smile directed at his ex-father-in-law so much, he might have found a little room to feel sorry for the guy.

But Seamus had sold her a bill of goods. Whether or not he'd done it at half the land value just to spite Trace, he'd outright lied about the place being livable.

"I trust your client records are more accurate," she continued smoothly. "I'll be opening again soon, so I'd like to have that information as quickly as possible."

Seamus's smile wilted a little. "Well, you know, with my daughter getting out of the hospital, I'm gonna be pretty busy helping her out and all."

"But, Grandpa, you told Nurse Courtney that Mom was going to be staying here." Drake's voice was curious. "Does that mean you're gonna stay here, too?"

Trace immediately shook his head. Just because he intended to be supportive of his ex-wife's recovery, it didn't have to follow that she needed to be under *his* roof while that transpired. And Seamus didn't, either, that was for damn sure. "No."

"Yes," Seamus said.

Ros broke the silence that ensued. "Well." She was expressionless as she looked from Seamus's beet-red face to Trace's. "I think this is my cue to exit and let you gentlemen sort things out."

She turned to Drake and gave him a soft smile. "I'm glad your mom is doing so well."

Then she walked past Trace and Seamus without a word.

She hesitated in the mudroom for a moment before pulling on Trace's favorite pair of boots.

They were much too big.

But damned if she didn't make it all look good as she strode out of his mudroom.

It was easy imagining her commanding attention inside a courtroom.

He looked back to find Seamus glaring at him.

Drake, on the other hand, just had a look on his face that was way too crafty for an eight-year-old kid. "Why was Ros wearing your shirt, Dad?"

Chapter Thirteen

"A cow is trying to break into my house."

Trace sat up and held the phone tighter to his ear. He'd fallen asleep on the couch. "Ros?"

She started again. "There is a *cow*—"

"I heard you." He looked blearily toward the window. Rain was streaking down the panes. But it was light.

Lighter than it should have been.

Usually he was up at least an hour earlier than this. Which is what he got for drinking himself into a stupor after having thc mother of all arguments with Seamus.

He cleared his throat. "Why d'you think she's breaking in?"

"Because she doesn't have a key?" Her tone was sarcastic. "Are you going to come and deal with this or should I call someone?"

He almost asked her who the heck she thought *that* would be? The local dogcatcher?

"I'll come," he said. His head pounded. He wasn't sure if he wanted to laugh from relief because she'd called him, or swear because she was obviously *not* happy.

He supposed a cow breaking in might do that to a person, but it was just as likely that she was still peeved from the evening before.

"I need to let Drake know," he told her.

"Fine." She ended the call and he hung his head for a minute. But there was no willing away the clanging going on between his ears.

He finally got off the couch and started the coffeemaker before going up to Drake's room.

His son was snoring away.

Trace left a note on the table next to his bed and went to his own room. A couple minutes with a bar of soap under a cold shower followed by clean clothes and he was driving up No Name Road with the coffee in his mug still too hot to drink and his wiper blades swishing.

The front door to Poocheez was closed.

And a calf was, in fact, there.

Maybe not trying to break in. But definitely gnawing away on the doorjamb as if it were his favorite salt lick.

He parked behind Ros's car, flipped up the collar of his jacket and pulled his hat down low over his face before stepping out into the rain. He yanked a rope from the box under his back seat. Then, with a blessedly minor amount of whistling and rope snapping, he drove the calf away from Poocheez. It splashed through the creek, skittering through the trees and off in the general direction where he belonged.

Unfortunately, Trace knew where one had gotten out, there were bound to be more. And maintaining fence in the rain was only slightly preferable to doing it in a snowstorm.

He coiled the rope, stuck it back in the box and glanced toward Poocheez.

Ros stood in the doorway, a woven blanket around her shoulders. She was still wearing the shirt she'd purloined from his closet. She might be scowling at him but he chose to take it as a good sign that she seemed to have slept in *his* shirt.

He decided that finding the fence break could wait a little longer.

"I've seen cows do some crazy things—" he crossed toward her "—but this one is right up there." He angled his head to study the freshly gnawed wood and rainwater streamed off his hat. "I don't think the door's any worse for wear. The jamb's looking pretty rough, though. I'll replace it."

"Before my grand opening if you don't mind." She closed the door in his face.

He grabbed the knob and, when he found it to be unlocked, stepped inside.

"I didn't say you could come in."

"You didn't lock the door, either."

She sniffed and looked at the array of fabric spread across her table. Despite the early hour, she was obviously sorting the pieces into piles by color. "Ever heard the term *trespass*?"

He pushed the door closed with the flat of his

hand. "I did not suggest to anyone that Sherry ought to stay at the Bar-H while she recovers."

"It's none of my business."

He slapped his hat against his thigh to shed the rest of the water from it. "You sure act like you're pissed off about it."

She slapped down a red square and glared at him. "I'm not...pissed off."

He couldn't help smiling a little.

She narrowed her eyes at him, let out a loud huff and walked around her blow-up bed to disappear through the doorway to the living area.

He followed, glancing at the fireplace as he passed it. "Smell is a lot better in there now," he commented as he stepped into the kitchen. "You need a fire going. Would warm things up." Just because it was July didn't mean it didn't get cold. Especially on a rainy morning. Especially around a frosty Rosalind Pastore. "I'll get firewood over here for you."

She jammed two slices of bread into a toaster that looked like it came out of a black-and-white television sitcom. "One more thing for me to owe you." She tightened her grip on the blanket.

He'd spent two hours the night before battling Seamus over things both new and old, all while trying to keep Drake from getting involved in any of it. Somewhere he had another fence down, it was raining buckets and his patience was thinner than usual.

"Seriously?"

Her mouth opened. Then closed. She'd moved her

little refrigerator into the kitchen. It looked almost comical sitting in the spot where the old, full-size one had been. She pulled out a carton of milk and set it on the counter. Then she slid it toward him with her index finger.

Apology by milk was a new one.

He thought briefly about his coffee. Still hot. But in his truck.

He opened the cupboard where he remembered she'd kept the glassware and pulled out the wineglass. He filled it and slid the milk carton back toward her.

Her expression wasn't quite as stern as she returned it to the minifridge. The toaster clicked then and the toast popped clean out of it. She caught the slices with practiced ease and dragged a butter knife through a jar of peanut butter. "Would you like a piece of toast?"

"Not with peanut butter," he said, watching her slather one of the slices. He'd never met anyone who liked peanut butter as much as Drake. Until now.

"You don't know what you're missing." She took a bite and licked a crumb from the corner of her lip.

Heat pooled at the base of his spine.

"I'll get things straightened out with Sherry," he said abruptly. He just wasn't exactly sure how yet. Right now, she couldn't manage any stairs, which left out her own second-story apartment regardless of whether Seamus was there with her or not. And once she could manage stairs, there was the matter of her brain injury that was affecting her hands. If she couldn't work, she couldn't afford rent on either the apartment or her hair studio. And now that Seamus had sunk all his money in his Mexico dream, he was no help—

"Like I said." Ros's voice was bland. "None of my business."

"And if I say I want it to be your business?"

She looked down at her toast. "I'd tell you to stop being ridiculous." Her voice sounded strangled. "We hardly know each other."

Despite everything, a bark of laughter escaped him, which only made his head pound even more.

He moved close enough that he could have whispered sweet nothings in the perfect shell of her ear if he wanted. "I know what every inch of you feels like." He reached around her and picked up her piece of toast. "What every inch tastes like."

The peanut butter was melting, oozing onto the napkin beneath it. He finished the slice in one bite and licked his thumb.

Her gaze flickered.

"No comment now?"

She slipped around him but he caught her hand and spun her back against him.

Her hands flattened on his jacket. "You're wet."

"Mmm-hmm." He kissed her temple and slid his hands beneath the blanket. Even through ancient blue denim, her nipples prodded his palms. "If you're cold, I know a good way to warm you up."

"This is too complicated. Sherry—"

"Is not the complication you think she is." He felt for the buttons between her breasts.

"Then Drake—"

"Adores you." He decided the buttons were too much work and just yanked the shirt apart.

She inhaled audibly. "Trace—"

He dragged his hand down her body, watching her pupils dilate. "Would you be quiet for a sec? I'm doing something important here."

Her head fell back slightly and she eyed him from beneath her lashes. "A *sec*?" She sounded breathless. Throaty. "That's all you got?"

He slid his hand between her thighs. "What d'you think?"

"I think—" she exhaled a soft moan that set his nerve endings on fire "—you better know how to sew on a bunch of buttons." She kissed him and he felt the curve of her smile against his lips. "Because I don't even know how to thread a needle."

He laughed softly.

Damn. He could love this woman.

The rain seemed set on staying.

Trace didn't mind.

His coffee was stone cold when he finally got back to his truck, but some things were worth a man's sacrifice.

Making love with Rosalind Pastore was most assuredly one of those things.

Discovering that her shower didn't work for squat was not. Especially when her gaze slid guiltily to the big stainless-steel dog-washing station in the grooming salon.

"*That's* what you've been using?"

"Don't sneer," she said, getting that expressionless expression on her face that might as well have been a flashing neon light signaling danger ahead. "There are worse alternatives. Once I get the leak in the shower fixed—"

"I'm going to strangle Seamus."

"Appealing thought, but somewhat illegal." She went to the dinky closet and pushed hangers around for a second before pulling out a black jacket. She slipped her arms into it and yanked the belt snug around her waist before flipping her hair free of the collar. "Don't worry. I've started calling around to plumbers." She picked up her purse and a stack of grand opening flyers. "Now are we going to Ruby's for breakfast or not?"

He nodded and jammed his hat on his head. They were picking up Drake on the way. When Trace had called him, he'd promised to be ready and waiting. "I can fix your pipes," he said.

Her eyebrows rose. "Yes, you've proven that very well."

He actually felt his neck get hot. Trace Powell, who hadn't blushed since he was eleven years old with his first crush on Susannah Blankenship. "Your shower pipe," he elaborated needlessly.

"If you really want to help me—" she pushed the flyers into his hands "—pass these out to everyone you know. I have a feeling Seamus's client list—if he ever produces it—won't be as helpful as I expected."

"Drake can probably tell you more about the clients he had than Seamus. He was the one doing the work." He grabbed the boots she'd taken from him the night before. He was happy to sacrifice a shirt to her—especially one that looked better on her than him—but he drew the line at the boots. Then he tucked the flyers under his jacket and they jogged through the rain to his truck.

It was a serviceable vehicle. A few years old. Spacious enough to keep him from feeling too hemmed in.

But it was miles away from the luxury of her car.

She didn't seem to pay any notice, though.

But then again, she'd been reduced to bathing in a freaking dog bath.

Yeah. He wanted to strangle Seamus Shaw for a whole bushel of reasons.

When they arrived at Ruby's, the restaurant was already filled to the gills.

Rain—even buckets of it—wasn't enough to stop people from crowding into the place. The clatter of plates and coffee mugs was almost as loud as the conversations and the jukebox.

More '70s-era music. Bubba the cook's doing, no doubt.

While Trace added his name to the wait list, Ros tacked a flyer on the bulletin board on the wall in the entryway. The woman in front of them noticed. "Poocheez is opening up again?"

Ros nodded. "Ten a.m. Last Saturday of the month. Do you have a dog?"

"My sister does. Tiny little thing. Bones wouldn't even make good soup stock. Y'oughta drop some flyers off at the vet's office," she suggested over her shoulder as she headed toward her table.

"Dad, there's Sammy Lee. Can I—" Drake shoved his Harry Potter book into Ros's hands and made a beeline toward his friend when Trace gave the okay.

"I think Sammy Lee might be more than just the soccer queen," Ros murmured, watching.

Trace realized Tina was the waitress serving Sammy Lee's table. Probably the real reason behind Drake's sudden interest.

A table finally freed up and they were seated. "Don't bother with the menu," Trace advised Ros when she opened it. "Order a cinnamon roll plus whatever Bubba's got on special."

"What if I don't like what he has on special?" She folded her hands atop the menu. "What if I want ancient grains or avocado toast?"

"Y'all don't want Bubba hearing that." A harried-looking waitress stopped at their table. "Three kinds of French. All of 'em good. But no avocado. As for grains, we got oatmeal. With fruit or without. But

Olivia'll be along soon to take your order. Meanwhile—" she held up her carafe "—coffee?"

Trace and Ros both turned their mugs right side up and the waitress filled them nearly to the rim.

"And a glass of milk, please," Ros called after her. Her gaze turned back to Trace. "What're you grinning about?"

"You."

Her lips twisted. "Good to know I'm a source of amusement."

"Honey, you're the source of a lot of things."

"Ros!" A pretty blonde sidled past the crowded tables. "I thought that was you." She smiled at Trace. "I'm Hayley."

Trace wondered if he was the only one who noticed the faint wilting in Ros's smile as she finished the introduction. "Trace Powell. My stepsister, Hayley Banyon."

He nudged an empty chair in invitation. "Want to join us?"

"Thanks, but I can't." Hayley glanced at her watch. "I just ran over between clients to grab a bite to go."

"Hayley's a family psychologist," Ros provided.

"Speaking of family, you *are* going to make it to Meredith's party on Satur—"

"Yes," Ros said a little too firmly. "I said I'd be there and I will."

"I'm so glad." Hayley's palm drifted to her stomach for just a second before she waved in acknowledgment when the waitress at the counter called out her name. "Don't tell anyone, but we're going to have lots of things to celebrate at the party." She winked and hurried over to retrieve her order.

"Did your sister just imply that she's—"

"I believe so." Ros's smile looked rueful. She rubbed her forehead and shook her head a little. "Birthday bonanza for Meredith."

"Don't like parties?"

"What can I say? I'm not a party kind of girl." She opened her menu again.

"Mornin', folks." Another waitress in a pink uniform dress set a glass of milk on the table. "I'm Olivia. D'you still need a few minutes or are you ready to order?"

Trace called Drake's name and gestured for him to come and sit.

"Bubba's special," Ros said, closing the menu. "And a, uh, a—"

"Cinnamon roll," Trace prompted. He didn't have to wait for Drake to know what his son would want. "Make it two more of the same."

"You got it." Olivia tucked her pencil behind her ear, collected the menus and went behind the counter. "Bubba, need three more hot," she yelled through the pass-through window to the kitchen.

Drake finally slid into his chair. "Sammy Lee's birthday party is next week. She invited me."

"Is everyone having a birthday this month?" Ros asked nobody in particular.

"Blame the weather," Trace said. "Gets pretty cold

around here in October. Folks need to do something to keep warm."

Drake reached for the milk. "I wanna go."

"To Sammy Lee's party?" Ros gave Trace a knowing look.

"Yeah." Drake gulped half the milk down. "I never knew she had a big sister." His gaze followed Tina as she sidled between customers. "And Sammy Lee's gonna have a bouncy house."

Ros scooted his book away from the milk glass. "You like bouncy houses, I guess?"

Drake's cheeks turned a little red and his gaze bounced off Trace's. "Yeah. Sure."

Trace buried his nose in his coffee mug.

Eight. And going on red-blooded male.

"So." Ros squared up her paper placemat with the edge of the table. "About Saturday night." She didn't look at Trace. "Would…ah…you be interested in going to a birthday party?"

It wasn't the first time he'd been asked out on a date by a woman. But it might as well have been, considering his stupefaction.

And he was aware that Drake was suddenly much more interested in their own table than he was with the other local attractions.

Trace wished like hell that he could say "yes."

But he couldn't.

"Sorry. I already have plans Saturday night. I wish I—"

"Don't worry about it," she said blithely. "It was

just a thought." She reached for her coffee and looked at Drake as if she had dismissed it already. "Do you know what you want to give Sammy Lee for her birthday present?"

Drake nodded. "A soccer ball," he said decisively.

Ros smiled. "And I have an idea how you can pay for it." She leaned toward him. "Helping me deliver flyers."

Trace might have been suddenly invisible for all the notice either one of them gave him at that point.

"How many and how much?" Drake asked.

"Two thousand flyers for—" she considered for a moment "—two cents each."

Drake rolled his eyes. "That's only forty bucks. Seven cents apiece."

"Five. *And* you give Sammy Lee some flowers along with the soccer ball."

"Flowers!" Drake wrinkled his nose. "Why?"

"Girls like flowers. Even soccer-playing girls. Do we have a deal?" She stuck her hand out over the table.

"Deal." Drake shook her hand.

Chapter Fourteen

Even though the rain continued, Ros and Drake began delivering flyers the very next day, working their way up and down the residential streets in Weaver, knocking on doors and handing them personally to whoever answered, whether they had a dog or not.

It was drudgework, and they got soaked, but she knew that Trace, who was trying to find and mend the latest break in his fence, had it worse.

At least she and Drake could use umbrellas.

They left flyers inside shops.

With the sheriff's office.

At the veterinarian's where a receptionist agreed to pass them on to their clients—but only after Ros proved she was up to their standards. "We can't go around recommending you to our clients if we haven't even seen what kind of a job you do," she pointed out reasonably, and pushed the stack of flyers Ros had set on the desk back at her.

Ros glanced around at the waiting room. Despite the weather, it was filled with clients, most of whom had a dog with them.

Only a couple had cats. And one person had a huge lizard in a cage.

"Send five clients over to me," she said impetuously. "I'll do them all for free. First thing tomorrow morning. Then you can decide."

The woman raised her eyebrows. "Any five?"

"Any five." Ros smiled confidently. "Send them my way—" she tapped the address on the flyer "—and I'll just leave this stack with you to pass out. Grand opening's a week from tomorrow."

Then she steered Drake back out into the rain and to her car, pretending she wasn't on the verge of hyperventilating. "You're going to be there tomorrow morning, right?"

"I dunno if I can. My mom—"

"Right." She swallowed the nervous knot rising in her chest. "She might be getting out of the hospital."

He nodded, but instead of looking elated as he ought to, he just gave Ros a concerned look.

"Are you going to be ready?" He shrugged almost apologetically. "You don't even got the sign finished yet."

"*I'll* be ready," she assured him as she backed out of the crowded parking lot. "Can't promise the sign will be. You have any friends with dogs? In fact, why don't you and your dad have a dog? Seems like every rancher should have a dog."

"We did. But he died a few years ago. He was really old."

"I'm sorry."

"Yeah." He sighed and swiped raindrops from his hair. "His name was Charlie. He was a good—" He broke off when the phone rang, sounding loud on the car's sound system.

Ros thumbed the button on her steering wheel as she braked for a jaywalker, umbrella tucked low over her head. "Hello?"

"Good afternoon," a woman's voice said. "I'm calling from Judge Taylor Potts's office for Rosalind Pastore."

Alarm skittered down her spine. "This is Rosalind Pastore."

"Please hold for the judge."

She wished she dared reach for her telephone so the conversation could be more private. She shot a glance at Drake and his eyes were wide.

"Are you in trouble?"

She managed a smile. "Of course not."

A new voice came over the speaker. "Ros. Taylor Potts. How are you?"

"In my car at the moment, Judge. So if I lose you, you'll know why."

"Understand completely. I'll be brief. We have an opening in the first judicial circuit and the nominating committee wants to submit your name."

Ros blinked. "What?"

"There'll be two others on the list, too, but what do you say? Are you interested in the bench?"

"I... I'm stunned actually." The car behind her tooted its horn and she realized the jaywalker had reached the sidewalk. She took her foot off the brake.

"Give it some thought. We're submitting the list to the governor next month and expect the decision shortly thereafter. If you could let me know within a few weeks, I'd appreciate it. Naturally, I hope you'll be interested, but if you're not, we'll need to move on to another candidate. You know how it is."

"Yes."

"Meanwhile, if you have any questions, give my office a call. Nice to hear your voice, Ros. I know it's been quite a year for you."

Her throat tightened. "Thanks for calling, Judge Potts. I—I'll be in touch."

She thumbed the button and Drake's music returned.

He was still looking at her. "What's the bench?"

"It means serving as a judge."

"Are you gonna do that?"

She shook her head automatically. "I'm opening up Poocheez. In fact—" she pointed toward the box sitting near his feet "—how many flyers are left?"

Drake riffled through it. "Thirty-two."

They'd started out with two packages of five hundred each. She had two more packages still unopened back at Poocheez, which she'd planned to distribute around Braden, but the rain had hampered their progress more than she'd expected.

"Let's forget about the flyers for now." It was hard to think straight with the way her brain was swirling.

"I want to stop at Shop-World instead. Then I'll get you back to your dad's in time for your grandpa to pick you up to see your mom this afternoon. Sound good?"

He nodded and looked out the window, tugging at his lower lip.

She drove through town, her windshield wipers capably keeping up with the rain, which had finally tapered from a downpour to a steady patter. The parking lot at the shopping center was as crowded as usual and Drake grabbed a cart on their way inside.

"What're you getting?"

Focus on one thing at a time.

"You need a soccer ball for Sammy Lee, don't you? Plus I need a birthday card for my mother's party tomorrow night."

"How old is she?"

"She'll be fifty-eight."

"If you married my dad would you guys have babies?"

She stopped dead in her tracks and another shopper nearly bumped right into them.

"Watch it, honey. Good way to get run over."

She mumbled an apology as she pulled the cart to one side of the aisle, pulling Drake along with it. She leaned toward him, lowering her voice. "What on earth made you ask a question like that?"

"You like him, don't you?"

Her lips moved but no words came out. Her swirling mind was now a total blank.

"You were wearing his shirt the other day. Grandpa says that's always a sign that a lady likes a man. So…?"

She straightened, feeling like a witness being cross-examined on the stand. "I *was* wearing his shirt," she allowed while not offering a single tidbit as to why that had been. "H-have you talked to your dad about this?"

He looked away.

"Drake?"

"He said he wasn't marrying anyone."

The way her stomach churned at that was something she'd think about later.

Maybe.

"There you go. And neither am I. And besides, your…your dad and I haven't known each other long at all."

Drake made a face, but he seemed willing to drop it. She nudged the shopping cart back into the wide aisle and they made their way to the sporting goods department where he selected one of the three soccer ball options available. He dropped the box in the cart and then helped her load a heavy package containing an unassembled bookcase on the bottom rack. The two of them finally steered the now-unwieldly cart to the greeting card section. Drake took far more time with his selection for Sammy Lee than she did plucking an impersonal birthday card from the shelf.

She thought about all the birthday cards her mother had given her over the years. All unique.

Many handmade. Not in the ugly Poocheez-sign way, either. And all accompanying a gift.

She stuck the card back on the shelf and chose one that at least had the word *Mother* on it.

She couldn't imagine presenting Meredith with a gift purchased from Shop-World, so she didn't try to find one. Once her mother heard that Ali and Hayley were both pregnant, anything anyone else gave her would be practically irrelevant, anyway.

With both birthday cards in the cart, they continued the trek through the enormous store. She added a variety pack of stencils from the craft department that she could use to paint the new sign and salivated just a little as they passed the entire row of microwaves on the way to the grocery side of the store. There, she added a bottle of inexpensive but adequate pinot noir and a gallon of milk. When they passed the eggs, she actually slowed.

Drake noticed. "Do you want a carton of eggs?"

She shook her head, even though she was uncharacteristically tempted. "I'd have to buy a pan, too, just to cook them."

Even if you returned to Cheyenne you would need to buy a pan.

She kicked a mental door closed on the voice in her head and added a box of saltine crackers and a fresh jar of peanut butter to the cart. "This, by the way—" she gestured at the contents "—is not an example of good dietary habits for you."

"No kidding," he agreed. "You don't got any fresh vegetables or nothing."

Feeling guilty, she grabbed a bag each of prewashed carrots and green apples on the way to the checkout. She didn't particularly like apples, but even they were palatable with a smear of peanut butter.

With everything paid for and tied inside plastic bags except for the bookshelf, they braved the rain again, loaded up the car and were soon on the highway out of town. As was Drake's habit, he flipped through the satellite stations nearly the entire way.

It might have been a little maddening if she wasn't so preoccupied.

"How's Azkaban coming?"

"I finished it."

She gave him a surprised look. "Already?"

"I read fast. And it was supergood, too. So." He tugged his lip for a moment. "If *I* wrote a book, would you read it? Even if it wasn't about wizards?"

"Sweetheart, I'd absolutely read anything you wrote."

He grinned and went back to flipping stations.

When they reached the Bar-H, the rain had slowed to a sprinkle and she could see Seamus sitting on one of the rocking chairs beneath the porch awning.

She reached behind her seat for the bag with the jug of milk and handed it to Drake. "That's for you and your dad."

"How're you gonna get that bookcase out of your trunk?" It had taken both of them to lift it.

"Don't worry. I'll manage it." She tucked the birthday card for Sammy Lee inside the bag with the milk.

"Thanks." With the soccer ball under one arm and the bag in his other hand, he loped toward the house, water splashing under his shoes.

Ros pressed the button to roll down the passenger side window and leaned over to look through it. "I hope you haven't been waiting long, Mr. Shaw," she called out.

"Just got here."

"Any progress on getting that list of clients together?"

Even across the distance she could see the way his face reddened. "Figured I'd get my injured daughter settled back t'home first."

His chastising tone slid off her back like rainwater off a duck. He'd owed the list to her well before Sherry's accident and he knew it. She'd just have more respect for the man if he'd admit he never had any plans to give her a single thing.

And she also knew that "t'home" in his opinion meant Trace's home.

If Trace and Seamus had come to an understanding on that point, Trace hadn't told her about it.

Not that he had to. Just because they'd slept together…

Would you guys have babies?

"Good luck at the hospital today," she told Seamus. Then she rolled up the window, turned around and headed back down to the highway.

She hit her phone button. "Call Nell," she told the car.

Nell answered on the third ring, sounding breathless. "You're not calling to cancel, are you?"

She ground her teeth a little. "No. I'm calling for a favor actually. I need a dog ASAP."

"Getting lonely living next to your studly neighbor?"

Ros didn't have time to get into *that*. She hadn't told Nell about sleeping with Trace and felt reluctant to do so now. It was too...private, she realized. Even to share with her oldest friend. "I have up to five dogs being sent over tomorrow morning by the vet in Weaver to test my competency as a groomer."

"Oh. Ouch. That's quick."

"They'll be a good referral for me if they're satisfied with the work. But I need some practice. At least to make sure I still remember how to do a basic wash and puppy cut, you know?"

"I'll bet. How long's it been since you volunteered at that animal shelter?"

"Don't remind me." Ros's voice was sharper than she intended. But her nerves had been ratcheting up since Taylor Potts's phone call. Drake's question hadn't helped. "Sorry. Just, uh, feeling the pinch of deadlines. My own fault entirely, though. I thought I'd have a few more days yet to get up to speed."

And Drake there to help and provide advice.

The absurdity of thinking of an eight-year-old boy as her consultant wasn't entirely lost on her, either. "So does anyone in the family have dogs? Nobody mentioned it when we were all together for dinner so I'm assuming not."

"Well, Meredith's allergic to dogs, so—"

"She is?"

"How did you not know that?"

"Because I'm as rotten a daughter as everyone thinks." She pressed her fingertip against the pain in her forehead. "What about friends? You and Archer know people, right?"

"You're not rotten," Nell chided. "And let me work on it for a few minutes." She hung up.

Ros turned onto the highway and then onto No Name Road. She thumbed the phone button again after debating for nearly two miles. "Call Trace."

He, too, answered on the third ring and didn't sound breathless at all.

Just sexy as all hell with his deep, "Hey, honey."

Whether he'd turned her down for tomorrow night's birthday party was moot. He still made flutters dance around inside her. "Where are you? Still out playing with the cows?"

"Yeah. Having a helluva good time. If I were a suspicious sort, I'd think someone had been deliberately pulling over fence posts. Instead, I know it's just a bunch of cows that love leaning. But at least the rain seems to have stopped. Get your flyers distributed?"

"Mostly. I dropped Drake off with Seamus a few minutes ago. Do you know anyone with a dog I can borrow for an hour or so this afternoon?"

"Probably. Why the rush?"

She told him about the vet.

"Let me work on it," he said, and hung up.

"Goodbye to you, too," she said to the empty car. Maybe it was living out in the boonies that somehow inspired abrupt endings to phone calls. "And by the way, I don't want to marry you, either."

Just saying the words made something ripple down her spine.

She parked in front of Poocheez, grabbed her purchases from the back seat and hurried to the front door. She'd deal with the bookcase box in her trunk soon enough.

Even though the rain had stopped, water still dripped off the roof onto her as she stood there unlocking the door.

What she needed was an awning for both the front door and the window.

Not if you keep your name on the circuit court list.

She burst inside and carried everything through to the kitchen. She stuffed her carrots and apples in the little fridge, filled the coffeemaker with a clean filter and fresh grounds and started it brewing, then returned to the grooming area.

She propped her hands on her hips, surveying it all.

Blow-up mattress. Mess of dog bandannas piled

on the grooming table. Toiletries stacked on the little corner shelf of the dog tub.

First things first.

She pulled the bedding off the mattress, which she then deflated enough to push through the doorway to the living area. She positioned it against the wall opposite the fireplace and set the pump to working to reinflate it while she went back into the kitchen where the coffeemaker was nearly finished gurgling.

She turned on the radio only to turn it back off again. She filled a coffee mug, added a splash of cream and sugar and carried it back into the grooming area.

The space was already much roomier without the mattress.

She moved her toiletries into the kitchen and moved dog shampoo back into place where it belonged. Fortunately, the canine toiletries were something that Seamus had believed in keeping stocked.

The air pump stopped pumping and she remade the bed, then stacked her books on the cardboard shipping box that had contained the dog shampoo. Drake might have finished his Harry Potter book already, but she still had fifty pages to go. Rereading for about the fiftieth time never diminished the comforting escape.

She rearranged the suitcases that she still needed to use for drawers because the dinky closet only held so much, and started a load of towels in the washer.

She folded the ones from the dryer and stacked them on another box she positioned next to the washing station. She filled the organizers from her suitcases that she'd already emptied with the bandannas, doggy barrettes and tiny rubber bands and lined them up on the shelves beneath the grooming table. She arranged scissors, combs and brushes inside the drawer, and was plugging in the kennel dryers when she noticed a truck driving up the road.

Two others followed.

She opened the door and leaned against the still-gnawed doorjamb and told herself she wasn't really getting choked up by the sight of her siblings climbing out of the vehicles. Every one of them had a dog with them.

Small.

Medium.

There was even a mammoth-size Great Dane riding in the back of Nell and Archer's truck.

"You ask and we deliver," Archer said as he lowered the tailgate for the horse-size dog to jump down.

Ros met Nell's gaze as she headed inside with a blanket covering Julia's baby carrier. "I can't believe you did this."

"Hayley's on her way, too. She just has to finish up with a patient first."

Ali, Greer and Maddie trooped through the door, too, and suddenly the grooming area was almost overflowing again.

Ros ceremoniously unfolded the webbed lawn

chairs that Trace had given her and pushed them toward Nell and Ali. Then she quickly went back to the kitchen to get the two chairs from the table that she'd moved back into the kitchen after deciding it wouldn't work as a reception desk no matter how she tried to position it. She set them next to the lawn chairs for Maddie and Greer.

Then she looked at Archer, who was standing just inside the doorway, while the Great Dane stood outside. She made a face at her stepbrother, then gave him a tight hug. "Thank you," she muttered.

He patted her back and pushed the leash into her hand. "Tiny here just needs a shampoo. I'm gonna wait in the truck." He cleared his throat. "Way too much estrogen in here."

Ros swiped her eyes, cleared her throat and looked from Tiny, who blocked the entire doorway, to her sisters. "All right, then. Who's first?"

"Me." Greer passed her the miniature ball of white fluff with eyes that she was holding in her right hand and took Tiny's leash. "This is Gretel. And this—" she held out the miniature ball of black fluff with eyes in her left hand "—is Hansel. They belong to Layla's preschool teacher and we need to get back to her in a little over an hour. So if that means just a wash and dry, that's what they get."

Ros lifted her chin away from the two slathering tongues. "Okay." She felt breathless as she placed Gretel into one of the kennel cages and carried Hansel over to the dog bath.

After that, it was just a blur of one wet dog after another, even more wet towels, loud blow dryers and buzzing clippers. She gave Hansel and Gretel pink and blue bandannas and quick matching poofs on top of their heads, a dignified black bandanna and trim for the schnauzer mix named Maxwell that Maddie told her belonged to Linc's secretary, a top knot and a purple tie-dye for the Pomeranian that Ali said belonged to her sergeant. Hayley arrived just as Greer and Maddie were leaving, with apologies for not having a dog with her. "But I brought brownies," she said, and everyone dove in except Ros because she was too busy. The studio was full of chatter and laughter and a lot of teasing where Archer was concerned because he resolutely remained in his truck throughout.

Ros had four relative successes so far if she didn't count scissoring Maxwell's beard a little shorter than she'd meant to. She was congratulating herself a little for her track record as she turned her attention away from Tiny for just a second to adjust the water pressure.

Congratulating herself was probably her downfall.

Tiny leaped straight out of the dog bath, suds and all, knocking Ros right on her butt. Then she bolted for the door just as Trace opened it to walk in, carrying a golden-haired cocker spaniel.

"Stop the dog!" Ros scrambled to her feet, but Nell was busy nursing Julia again, Hayley and Ali were snooping in her kitchen and Trace didn't move quite fast enough to grab Tiny as she plowed into him and out the door.

Ros nearly collided with him, too, as she chased the dog outside and he followed.

Tiny suddenly stopped short when Archer got out of his truck.

The three of them had the dog cornered and the cocker spaniel in Trace's arms started yapping.

Ros pulled the bag of treats from the pocket of the too-large smock she'd put on after getting her shirt soaked by Hansel and Gretel and poured several into her palm. "Come on, Tiny. Have a treat." She tossed two onto the sidewalk directly in front of the dog.

Tiny snatched up the morsels and sat on her haunches, looking bored despite the suds running in rivulets down her gleaming gray coat.

Ros tossed a few more treats out, hoping to coax the dog back toward her. Or at least to prevent Tiny from bolting as Ros inched closer to her. "Did you just happen to have the owner of Wyoming's largest Great Dane on speed dial?" she asked Archer.

He looked amused over the entire situation, which was typical of him. "She's Taylor Potts's dog."

Ros shot him a look. "You know Taylor?" Stupid question. Archer knew the entire who's who of the legal community in Wyoming, Colorado and Montana.

"He dated her," Nell said from behind her. "You know. Before he came to his senses and married me."

"Who is Taylor?" Trace was trying to shush the

spaniel, who was barking louder than ever, probably because Tiny was getting treats and he wasn't.

"A judge from Cheyenne," Ros muttered, and offered Trace several treats in her outstretched palm.

He scooped them up and fed them to the yapper, who immediately chowed them down.

"She's been in Braden for the past few weeks covering for Sweeney, who's been out sick," Archer was saying.

Ros looked back at him and the Great Dane sitting between them. "I s'pose you had something to do with her call?"

"Taylor called you?" He looked genuinely surprised, and she wished she hadn't said a word.

She dumped the remaining contents of the treat pouch on the ground. As soon as Tiny leaned forward to get them, she sprang forward and grabbed the dog's collar.

Tiny gave her arm a lick after wolfing down the treats as if nothing was amiss at all and strolled alongside Ros toward the door.

She was breathless, and aware that she looked a mess by that point, but she stopped next to Trace. His beard had already grown back again, looking as thick and dark as the first time they'd met.

She knew she was smiling up at him like some total goof but couldn't help it. "You came, too."

He thumbed back his hat an inch, studying the situation with a rueful expression. "Doesn't look like you needed me."

"Looks can be deceiving." Her fingers slipped and she almost lost control of the dog collar again. "Tiny, sit," she commanded firmly, and miracle of miracles, the dog sat. Promptly. "And who is this?" She scrubbed her fingers over the dog he was holding.

"Freckles. Belongs to Rodney's mom. But if you don't need more practice, don't sweat it. She won't mind missing out on a free dog shampoo."

"Are you kidding?" She tucked her arm through Trace's and pulled him along with Tiny back inside Poocheez. "The more, the merrier."

And she didn't even care about the openly speculative looks she earned from Nell and all the rest.

Chapter Fifteen

By the next night at Meredith's party, however, being the source of continued speculation among her family members was starting to wear thin.

If one more person asked her why her boyfriend hadn't come to the party she would scream.

First, Trace was not her boyfriend.

Secondly, she'd never suggested to anyone—except him—that she'd wanted to bring a guest to the party.

"I hear you had a trial by fire yesterday afternoon." Carter appeared out of the dark and sat beside Ros where she'd sought sanctuary on the filigreed garden bench in their backyard. All around her, tiny white lights flickered among the bushes and trees. "How'd it go with the dogs the vet lined up this morning?"

Ros toyed with her wineglass. She'd been nursing the same drink all evening. "I think it went well. It was less exciting than yesterday at any rate. No Marmadukian escapees."

He chuckled. "Archer told us about that. Sounds like it was quite a sight. You all right out here?"

"Yeah. Just needed a breather after all those gifts."

Chief among them, Ali's and Hayley's independent announcements of being pregnant that had spurred Meredith to dance a jig with them right there in the middle of the house.

She looked through the windows at the crowd inside. "I guess I didn't realize there'd be so many guests." In addition to their family, Carter's brother David and his entire crew were there as well. Plus there were a lot of faces that she didn't know at all.

"Your mother has a lot of friends."

"And *your* mother is quite a character." She could see Vivian Templeton now through the window. Almost as petite as Meredith was, the silver-haired woman seemed in her element, thoroughly enjoying herself whether or not she still had a contentious relationship with her own sons.

Carter grunted slightly. "That's one way to describe Vivian. You've met her before tonight, though."

"Yes. I don't think I impressed her much." Vivian was rich from Pennsylvania steel money, and more opinionated than any ten people combined.

"That's okay," he said dryly. "I never impressed her much, either." Then he shifted as if to leave, but he didn't. "It means a lot to Meredith and me that you came tonight, Ros. And not just tonight, either. I know this hasn't been an easy year for you. Your father—"

She stiffened. "Carter just…wait."

"I understand. You don't want to talk about him. Particularly to me."

She stared down at a brick painted to look like a big yellow butterfly. Probably her mother's work. "Nell told me about…about what he did. To my mother."

He was silent for a long moment.

Inside the house, there was a loud burst of laughter and catcalls.

"How much did she tell you?"

Ros's mouth felt dry and the bracing sip of wine she took didn't help any. "Enough to know that *you* weren't the reason she left us." Her pulse pounded in her head. "I'm sorry for…well…for blaming you all these years."

He sighed deeply. "You should hear how many years I've blamed my mother for things, too. You don't have anything to be sorry for."

"Nell said I should hear the whole story from my mother."

"Nell's right." He stood and extended his hand. "Telling you has only ever been Meredith's decision to make."

"I don't mean right now," she said, alarmed.

"I know that." His hand didn't move. "It's just time for cake."

"Oh. Well." Feeling foolish, she put her hand in his and realized it was probably the first time in her life that she'd done so. He pulled her to her feet and they left the bower of fairy lights to return to the house.

Maddie was just lighting the candles on the wide

slab of cake decorated with daisies that had been placed in the middle of the dining room table.

"Do we have the fire department on standby?" Meredith joked.

"No, but I've got them on speed dial," Ali replied. "Go on. Make a wish."

Meredith gazed at Ros, then Carter, and her eyes sparkled. "Some wishes don't need candles to come true. Now come." She tugged Ali next to her. "Carter, you have your camera ready? I want a picture with all my children here. Archer. Hayley?" They moved to stand behind her along with Maddie and Greer. "Rosalind."

Ros joined them, intending to stand behind Meredith, too, but her mother snaked her arm around Ros's waist and pulled her next to her.

"Everybody say *Limburger*."

"Dad joke," Ali jeered. Carter snapped the picture with his phone as Meredith leaned over, blowing out the candles.

"Make sure you send it to everyone," Meredith told him.

"Yes, dear." He was busy typing on his cell phone, and a moment later, various pings sounded throughout the room.

Ros glanced at her phone when the notification chimed, but instead of Carter's name showing up, it was Drake's.

She'd missed his call ten minutes earlier while she'd been outside. She couldn't help feeling a sharp pang and dialed him back even though it was getting late. She slipped through the crowd of people and into Carter's office where it was quieter.

"Ros!" Drake sounded elated when he answered and she let out a relieved breath.

"I saw you called. What's up?"

"My mom's getting out of the hospital tonight! We're just waiting for some doctor to sign something."

"That's great, honey." She braced herself. "Are you and your dad taking her home to your house?"

"Dad's not here. He's got friends over tonight. You remember. The veterans I told you about?"

"Oh. Right." Realizing that Trace really did have a prior commitment made something inside her feel better.

"Are you still at your mom's birthday party?"

"I am. In fact, I probably should get back to it. But I'm glad you called to tell me your good news. And hey. The dogs this morning went fine so the veterinarian is going to keep our flyers around for their clients."

"Cool."

Nell called her from over her shoulder. "Ros—"

She glanced back at her friend.

"You're missing cake," she mouthed.

Ros nodded and started toward her. "I'll talk to you later," she said into the phone. "Okay?"

"'Kay. Be careful when you drive home."

"I will." She slid her phone into the pocket of her

palazzo pants and tucked her arm through Nell's as they returned to the others. "Who'd you find to babysit Julia tonight, anyway?"

"One of the women from Archer's office. She has two kids of her own. Was that Trace?"

"Drake. He wanted to tell me his mom is being released from the hospital."

"That's good news. Is she going to be staying with them?"

"No idea."

"Have you just *asked* Trace?"

"It's none of my business."

Nell gave her a sidelong look. "You're sleeping with him, aren't you? And don't start shaking your head like that. I've known you too long."

Ros shrugged. "It's just sex."

"Right. I saw your face when you looked at him yesterday. And Hayley told me about seeing the three of you at Ruby's the other morning. You're crazy about those Powell boys."

"Crazy fades."

"How do you know?" Nell challenged bluntly as they rejoined the others. She picked up a plate with a neat square of cake on it and pushed it into Ros's hands. "The only things you've ever been crazy about were the law and peanut butter."

If they hadn't just rejoined the rest of the party, Ros might have told her about the judge's phone call. But after that, there was no good opportunity.

They ate cake and toasted Meredith. More wine

was poured, and chaos erupted all over again when guests started departing.

"I'm going to go, too." Ros stopped next to her mother after seeing Nell and Archer out the door.

"Wait," Meredith said. "Please." Her eyes searched Ros's. "Carter said you might want to…talk."

Ros felt an edge of panic. "It's your birthday. There'll be another time—"

Meredith squeezed her arm. "Just wait," she said again.

So Ros waited.

But the evening dragged out even longer because David and his wife, Season, lingered after everyone else had left, so Ros went back out to sit on the garden bench again. She stared at her phone, her thumb hovering over Trace's phone number.

It was nearly midnight. If she called him now, would he answer? Or would he still be with his buddies? Or making sure his ex-wife was comfortably settled in his house?

She sighed and, before she could talk herself out of it, hit *Dial*.

His phone didn't even ring, though. It just went straight to his voice mail. *Leave a message*, his deep voice said, and then the tone sounded.

She didn't know what to say in a message any more than she knew what she would have said to him had he answered. "It's Ros," she said abruptly. "Nothing important. Just, uh—" *wanted to hear your voice* "—just wanted to remind you the doorjamb still needs to be replaced at Poocheez." She hung up and dropped her head onto her hand.

What a monumental idiot.

She pushed off the garden bench and went inside the house. Meredith and Season were still in close conversation and there was no sign of David and Carter at all.

She found her purse in the bedroom she'd used during her dreaded enforced visitations to her mother's house and let herself quietly out the front door.

She stopped to buy a coffee at an all-night convenience store and then drove back to Poocheez.

After letting herself in, she wandered through the grooming area. The stainless steel sparkled. The waist-high bookcase she'd bought at Shop-World and assembled herself stood near the front door, filling the role of a perfectly adequate reception counter as well as a retail space to display items for sale. There were dog treats, collars and chew toys. All things that she'd found on Seamus's storage shelves even though she'd seen in his ledger books that he'd only ever made a lackadaisical effort in sales.

And then there was the waiting area.

Two kitchen table chairs. Two woven-webbed lawn chairs.

She folded both, tucked them under her arm and went through the doorway to the living area, snapping off the light and closing the door behind her.

Then she opened her bottle of wine, poured a glass and carried the chairs outside with her. She opened them both, sitting in one and propping her feet on the other.

An endless black expanse studded with stars spread out before her.

It was beautiful.

But was it home?

She was no closer to an answer when she reached the bottom of the wineglass and leaned over to pour another glass. That's when she saw Trace.

Leaning against the corner of the building just watching her.

She ought to have been startled. She wasn't.

"It's late," she said.

"I figured I'd better get that doorjamb fixed."

"You know I didn't mean it."

"I know." His boot scraped against the brick pavers as he crossed to her. He tossed his hat and it landed neatly on the table with the umbrella.

"Is your ex-wife home?"

"I set her up in my mom's old bedroom. It's on the first floor. No steps. Seamus is on the couch. Drake's in his bed. There's no other choice. Seamus's money is sunk into a Mexican beach and mine's tied up in the Bar-H. Sherry can't afford one of those skilled nursing places to finish her recovery and either Seamus stays there to help her, or I do. She prefers her dad over me, and I can't say I blame her. It's temporary, Ros. Just until the insurance mess gets worked out."

Her throat tightened. "And what's this?"

"She's there. And I'm here. You tell me."

"I don't know," she whispered.

"I'm *here*," he repeated quietly.

"For how long?"

"That's the question I should be asking you."

"What do you mean?" But even when she asked the question she knew.

He lifted her bare feet to sit in the chair, but held on to her ankles when she would have pulled them away. "Drake told me about the call you got from that judge."

"It's just my name on a list for the circuit court."

"In Cheyenne. Did you think Drake wouldn't be curious about what the 'first judicial' meant?"

"Yes, in Cheyenne," she admitted. "But it doesn't mean the governor would appoint me to the vacancy. There'd be two other candidates with just as much a chance."

"But if the governor did?"

"I'd serve for a year and have to be reelected to retain the position. Assuming that occurred, it's a four-year term after that. But it doesn't matter, because I'm going to tell Judge Potts I'm not interested."

"Why?"

"Because I'm here. I'm not a lawyer." She tried shifting again, but he still held her feet in his hands.

"Evidently you *are* if the nominating commission wants your name on the governor's list."

"And if I go, you can buy back your land. Because I can't very well be both a full-time judge in

Cheyenne and run Poocheez out here at the end of No Name Road."

"This isn't about the land. It's about you. And what you want."

"What I want is to just get on with my life and forget everything else that's happened before now!"

"Yeah." He sounded weary. "Been there." He rubbed his thumbs over her arches. "It's a lot easier to go forward when you're not dragging the weight of your past along with you."

"I'm not dragging any weight."

"You sure about that?" His warm hands surrounded her feet. "What about all that business with your father?"

Ros went still.

"I was curious, you know. Why a woman like you would end up in a place like this. Pastore isn't a particularly common name. Start looking and all kinds of information comes up where the Pastore name is concerned."

"I wish you hadn't done that."

"Would you have told me that your father was sitting in the state penitentiary?" He didn't wait for an answer. "You wouldn't have. Because you're busy pretending you can forget about it all."

"You don't know me well enough to—"

"I know plenty. You're not the kind of person who sits around and lets life happen to her. Whatever lands in your lap, you deal with it."

"I did deal with it." She finally managed to yank her legs free. "I bought *Poocheez*."

"And running a place like this is what you've wanted to do your entire life? Ros, when it comes to the past, you're not dealing with jack sh—"

"And herding cows and fixing fence is what you've wanted to do *your* entire life, gunny?" She pushed out of her chair and jabbed her finger in the air between them. "What about those sixteen years with the marines? What about the past *you* drag around with you?"

"There's the difference, honey. When I was in the military, this place was the past I was dragging around. And I don't mean only Drake. I mean all of that." He swept out his arm. "The land. The Bar-H. My history. The fact that my mother, instead of admitting to me that she needed help, would sooner sell off chunks of land to pay the taxes. Land that my father had drunk himself to death over trying to maintain the way *his* father had done.

"The crap that happened when I was serving? Making peace with that was a helluva lot easier than making my peace with *here*. With learning to separate the man I wanted to be from the man I'd been. Not to let the Bar-H turn me into my father. And not to be a gunnery sergeant version of a father to Drake even though I knew a helluva lot more about being a gunny than I did anything else."

He stood, too, and swept up his cowboy hat. "This is the man I am, Ros. Father first. Rancher second.

Gunny to a bunch of military vets from twenty-two to seventy-two who get together once a month in my garage to shoot the shit and work out their variety of nightmares that *they're* still dragging around."

He jammed the hat down on his head looking as if he were ready to turn on his boot heel and walk away.

She didn't want him to leave. "What kind of nightmares?"

"Does it matter? All of ours. We burn off steam. Play poker. Pound away on an old truck of my dad's. Sometimes we talk about the past. For some it's the good ol' days. For some, it's anything but good."

"What was your nightmare?"

He didn't even hesitate. "The kid I couldn't save. Not from the fighting. But from his own demons. Kids like Rodney's brother. Kids like I never want to see Drake turn out to be." He lifted his arms slightly. "If that means showing him that I care enough about the welfare of his mother even after the wringer we put each other through, then that's what I'll do. God knows it's more than my father ever taught me."

He stepped back to her and lifted her chin. "Sometimes the only way forward is to go back first, Ros. I know where I've been. I know who I am. What I am. And I know who I want. Problem is, I don't think she knows at all."

Her chest ached. "You told Drake you weren't marrying anyone."

"So did you! And yeah, he told me. He tells me

everything, whether I'm ready to hear it or not. Hell, it wasn't even a month ago that you and I sat right here in this very place and you told me that sort of thing wasn't your style."

"Exactly. It wasn't even a month ago! I don't… This isn't—"

"Logical? Sensible? In Rosalind Pastore's world there is a timeline for falling in love with someone?"

She felt hollowed out. "Nobody said anything about love."

He brushed his thumb down her cheek and stepped away again. "I just did. Sherry and I were kids playing at real life and that was bad enough to get through. You? You're the kind of woman I'm not sure I could survive losing. And I damn sure don't want Drake yanked to pieces when he's already crazy about you."

"I would never intentionally hurt Drake."

"Letting him think this is the life you want and leaving when you realize it's not?" He shook his head. "You want to get on with your life? Figure out what you're running from first. Once you do—" he leaned down and kissed her softly "—you know where I'll be."

He turned on his heel and walked away.

Chapter Sixteen

It was the buzzing that woke her.

Loud. Noisy. Practically vibrating right through the ground beneath Ros's blow-up mattress.

She rolled to her feet and peered bleary-eyed at her phone.

Nine a.m.

She hadn't gotten to sleep until dawn after Trace left her feeling emotionally wrecked. And now, it sounded as if someone was steamrolling outside her very door.

She blindly yanked a shawl out of the suitcase and wrapped it around her shoulders as she hurried through the grooming area. Snatching aside the sheet over the window, she looked out only to shriek in alarm when a massive blast of water sprayed across the glass.

But the window didn't break. She didn't get drenched. And the spray continued onward, leaving behind dirty rivers running down the glass. She peered through them and saw the increasingly familiar trucks lined up behind her car.

She winced again when the hard spray of water passed over the window once more and let the sheet fall back into place. Then she hurried back through the living area, pushing her feet into her tennis shoes along the way, and went out the kitchen door to see Carter wielding a chain saw against the overgrown cottonwood in the graveyard. The massive pile of weeds was obviously due to Meredith, who was attacking them with a hoe, her gauzy scarlet skirt swishing with every hack.

They were both so busy they didn't even notice Ros when she walked around the building to the front side of it.

Archer was behind the massive power-washer that he was spraying over the front of the building and Nell was planting flowers in the ground around the tree while Julia lay on a blanket in the shade.

Ros blinked hard and gave Archer a wide berth as she passed him. When he saw her, his lips twisted in a mischievous smile.

"Don't you dare," she yelled above the noise of the machine, and hurriedly ran over to where Nell and Julia were. He *surely* wouldn't turn the water on her there.

She just saw him laugh and continue working the powerful fan of water back and forth across the building.

Which was…clean.

She was so surprised she stopped and stared.

No longer the color of *blech*, the siding was a bright, clear white.

"Amazing what a power wash can do, isn't it?"

She looked over at Nell, who was sitting back on her knees, a trowel in her gloved hand.

"Amazing what you guys can do." Ros spread her arms. "What is all this? Was this your idea?"

"Your mother's," Archer said, cutting off the motor in time to hear. Water dripped from the eaves with loud plops. "She bribed us to come out here and help clean up the place. She said there'd be pancakes, bacon and leftover birthday cake. And yet what do we find? You so dead to the world you don't even answer the door when we knock." He shook his head dolefully.

"I don't have pancakes and bacon, much less something to cook them with," Ros said. She couldn't resist Julia, looking precious in a sunny yellow romper, and picked her up for a cuddle. "On the bright side, though, I have lots of paper plates. So if Meredith has the cake, you'll be good."

"Ye of little faith. Your mom brought everything we need. And—" He pointed the long wand in his hand toward the trucks and a stack of packing boxes she hadn't noticed. "Ali's been going around pilfering all of our kitchens for stuff. She said you didn't have diddly. And Grant's on his way with a grown-up-size refrigerator."

"I can't afford a refrigerator."

"He's got a connection with a guy who refurbishes appliances."

She closed her eyes for a moment, and felt a faint laugh rise in her. Or maybe it was a tinge of hysteria. "As long as it's not the toxic fridge coming back to haunt me."

"Arch, help get—oh, good, Ros. You're up." Carter had appeared around the corner of the building carrying one of the heavy patio chairs from the back. "Your mom thought the furniture would be good in the front here. Give your customers another place to sit."

Would she even have real customers?

Handing out a bunch of flyers didn't guarantee anything.

Did she even want real customers?

She wanted to damn Trace for putting the idea into her head, but honesty wouldn't let her.

She moistened her lips. "Sounds great. I'm, uh, going to get dressed."

She scurried back into the building, brushed her teeth, washed her face and twisted her hair into a messy knot. Then, nightshirt exchanged for leggings and a tank top, she went back outside.

If her family were going to make Poocheez look presentable, she'd do nothing less than her part, too.

"No, no. You just need a *drop* of water on the griddle. Too much water and it ends up cooling it off." Meredith swiped away Ros's puddle of water with the corner of a clean towel and demonstrated with a flick of her fingers. "See how it sizzles? All you're doing is making sure it's hot enough for the pancake batter. And it is, so..." She handed Ros the mixing bowl. "Now you just pour a bit out until you have the size pancake you want and wait for it to stop bubbling. Then you'll know it's time to flip."

Ros tucked her tongue between her teeth and concentrated on pouring the batter out onto the flat griddle that spread across two burners of her stove. Some of the pancakes ended up more oblong than circular and they were all different sizes, but she didn't spill anything. And when all was said and done, only two pancakes ended up in the trash.

She cooked the bacon—not cheater style—to a near-perfect crisp in the oven and even made a half dozen scrambled eggs that Archer and Grant alone rapidly consumed.

And now she had a proper-size nontoxic refrigerator in her kitchen. A small microwave on the counter. Real forks and knives and spoons in her drawer, and real plates.

They used them for the pancakes and bacon, which they ate outside, sitting around the patio table that had been moved to the front of Poocheez where they could admire the newly cleaned siding and sparklingly clear picture window.

"You need awnings," Meredith said. "Over the door and the window."

Ros bit back a smile. "Maybe someday I'll be able to order them."

"Oh, Carter can build the frames," her mother said easily. "Then we'll just cover them with weather-resistant fabric. They make it in a million styles. We could make curtains for inside the window, too. But just having an awning will help with the sun shining through it. I bet it gets hot."

"It does, but you probably should make sure Carter knows you're volunteering his services first." As soon as they'd finished eating, her stepfather and Grant had disappeared inside the house with piles of wood and all sorts of tools.

Frankly, Ros had been a little too alarmed to ask what exactly their intentions were, and she'd been relieved when Meredith said they were fixing the shower leak.

Nell and Archer had taken Julia home and Ali'd had to report to duty, which left Meredith and Ros alone.

"One thing Carter is very used to is my volunteering him for one thing or another. And he'd do anything for our girls. That includes you, in case you needed to be told."

"I know." She flicked a fly away from her arm. "It's nice that Maddie is able to watch Reid for Grant and Ali."

"They're always shuffling their kids around, watching whoever needs watching. Frankly, I don't get to babysit nearly as often as I'd like." Meredith leaned back against the table and crossed her ankles. She tilted her head back and her curly hair reached almost to her elbows. She was wearing a tank top similar to Ros's, only Meredith's was a swirl of purple and blue. "What a lovely day it is. All washed clean from a summer rain."

"I'm sorry I walked out last night without saying goodbye."

Her mother waved a dismissive hand. "Season was talking about Delia. She worries about her so."

Delia was Season and David's youngest, pretty much the same age as the triplets. "I thought she worked for Vivian these days."

"She does. But she had a bit of a crush on someone that didn't work out. You know Delia, though. She's grown up always having a bit of a crush on someone. She just hasn't met the right one yet. When she does…" Her mother smiled. "Life will change for her the way it does for all of us."

"How do you know you've met the right one?"

Her mother slid a glance her way. "Are you speaking personally, or—"

Ros could hardly bear to think about Trace. "You probably thought you'd met the right one when you married my father," she said, changing tack.

"Oh, Martin," her mother said on a sigh. "I was very young. No family of my own. And he was very charismatic. I mistook his excessive ambition as passion for life, I think. I realized too late that the things he said he loved about me were the things he felt driven to change. Carter's different."

"He doesn't beat you," Ros said flatly.

"I don't mean just that," her mother said mildly. She didn't seem jarred by Ros's bold jump into those black waters. "People always say how different Carter and I are. He's rules and order and I'm anything but. Carter says I bring music to his life. That's why he gave me this." She unfastened her anklet and the tiny bells jangled softly as she set it on the table between them. "Before we were even married. So I would always know that he wanted to give me music, too."

Ros wasn't looking at the anklet, though. She was looking at the small raised scars that had been concealed by the piece of jewelry. White. Jagged. But still legible. *M.P.* Repeated around her entire ankle.

Scars Ros had never before seen. Ever.

Because her mother had always worn the musical ankle bracelet that hid them.

"Martin did that with the pocketknife I'd given him as a wedding gift." Her mother's voice was quiet. "He wanted to make sure I never forgot that I belonged to him."

"I don't know what to say." Ros's throat was so tight it ached. "You could have them removed. I know someone who's helped clients of mine remove old tattoos. Maybe the scars could be lasered—"

"I didn't need to have them removed." Her mother watched her carefully. "And I couldn't remove the cigarette burns, anyway. I don't know how much Nell told you about those. Do you want to see them, too?"

Ros shook her head. Her mother's arms and shoulders were bare from the sleeveless tie-dyed top she wore with her gauzy skirt. Wherever the burns were, Martin had made sure they weren't easily visible.

"Carter is the one who encouraged me to leave

him," Meredith said huskily. "At first he was just this very nice man—a little severe and very solemn—who worked at the same place where I was a file clerk. Part-time because Martin wanted me to focus on our family. That was his claim, anyway. He could barely tolerate my working at all but did so in the early days for the sake of appearances."

"He didn't want you to gain independence."

"Hindsight makes it easy for me to recognize that. The romantic blush had already worn off by then since he accused me of flirting with any man I happened to encounter and punished me accordingly. He'd switched to less obvious methods by then."

"Cigarettes instead of pocketknives."

She nodded. "One afternoon, I was sick in the break room. One of the burns was infected. Carter found me." Her eyes met Ros's. "I tried not to fall for him. I knew it was wrong. But—" Her throat worked, and she exhaled. "He wanted to take us away from Cheyenne. Archer and Hayley were still young. It hadn't been that long since they'd lost their mother. He said we could go as far away as we needed to keep us safe. But I knew that Martin would never let me leave with you. Never." She twisted her ankle around. "I'd tried when you were only a few weeks old and got those as a result. So Carter moved away and I stayed," she said quietly. "Three more years."

"Because of me."

"You were my baby. I couldn't leave you."

Ros pushed away from the table and paced toward

the flowers that Nell had planted, then back again. "But you did leave me. In the end, that's exactly what you did." A lifetime of feeling second-best where her mother was concerned churned inside her chest. She gestured at the building. "No amount of awnings now are going to make up for that fact."

"And I can tell you why and hope you'll find some understanding, or we can go on just as we are now. But don't make the mistake of thinking that I didn't love you. Or that it didn't break something inside me." Her mother's eyes glistened, but she didn't flinch or look away.

Ros was the one who did that. She swallowed and looked down at her shoes through her own tears and after a long moment, her mother continued.

"You had just had your third birthday. Martin went all out for it. A clown that terrified you. A pony that didn't." She swiped her hair away from her cheek. "I ran into Carter again. He was in town on business. Turned out that he hadn't moved very far. Just from Cheyenne to Braden where his brother lived. And—" She finally looked away to the anklet she held between her fingers. "Carter was still everything that was right. And good. And when he took me in his arms, I knew that he was my home."

Ros started.

"Just like that," her mother said softly. "Home. Anyway we never expected to get pregnant. But I knew I couldn't stay with Martin after that. I packed your favorite things in a bag and we were sneaking out through the kitchen when Martin came in. We fought over you and I—" She cleared her throat.

"You knocked him out cold with a cast-iron frying pan," Carter said from the doorway. "And the two of you came to me."

Meredith held out her hand to him and he took it in his and kissed it. Then he looked at Ros. "Martin had a concussion," he said quietly. "But he already had clout. Politically. Professionally. Your mom was charged with aggravated assault and put in jail, and you landed right back in Martin's arms where he wanted you."

Ros stared at her mother. Horror and astonishment vied for the upper hand. "The charges didn't stick." There was no way she wouldn't have known about it if they had.

"Only because Carter had insisted on photographing my injuries back when we'd first met in Cheyenne." Meredith pressed his hand to her cheek. "And he still had the photos three years later."

"You leveraged the photos to force my father to drop the charges," she realized aloud.

Carter nodded. "But he still had physical custody of you. And he wasn't going to give you up. He'd already had one of his judicial cronies sign a court order that your mother was an unfit parent."

"We had proof he'd abused me," Meredith said. "Martin had proof of my infidelity. I was pregnant with Carter's babies. He'd just started his own firm.

Back then reputations were everything. No matter which way I turned—"

"You had impossible choices," Ros finished. She pinched the bridge of her nose until the burning behind her eyes receded again. "That's why he never left the state," she murmured. "When people wanted my father to run for office. To aim higher than just Pastore Legal. *The People's Champion.*" She practically spit the words. "He had to keep me here in Wyoming because you made him."

"We saw you regularly." Meredith's voice thickened. "We knew he never laid a hand on you. Unlike me, you were his shining joy."

"We served Martin with custody papers again when you were fourteen," Carter went on. "In turn, he filed papers disavowing you as his child. Severing his parental rights altogether. Your mother couldn't get you because of the order still in place that we were also trying to overturn with the custody papers. You could have been stuck in foster care for who knows how long while we tried to untangle his lies."

Ros swayed and took a steadying step.

"He withdrew his filing when we withdrew ours," Carter finished.

"Martin was your hero." Meredith wasn't bothering to hide her tears. "He'd already taken away so much, how could I take that away from you as well? I knew you hated me. I didn't want you to hate the only other parent you had. As long as we kept this horrible...détente...you were safe."

Ros felt sick inside. "You should have told me."

"When?" Meredith stood and held out her palms helplessly. "When would it have been better to tell you any of these things about the man you idolized? When you were sixteen and Nell had begun living with you? When you passed the bar and joined Pastore Legal, which had been your dream for most of your life? Or when you were thirty-six and you discovered the feet of clay that he truly had?"

"If his other crimes hadn't come to light, you wouldn't even be here right now," Carter said. "You'd still be at Pastore Legal legitimately championing the things that Martin only claimed to espouse. You were the real deal, Rosalind. We all knew that. Martin most particularly, I'm sure."

"Didn't stop him from ruining my life, though, did it?"

Her mother covered Ros's shoulders with her hands. "Your life is *not* ruined," she said huskily. "You have the same things you've always had. People who love you. A mind that is frighteningly fierce and a heart that has an incredible capacity to care about others."

"I don't know how you can say that, when I've done so little to prove it to you."

"Sweetheart." Her mom cupped her cheek. "I wish you could see yourself the way I do. Such a beautiful, accomplished woman. Who is always going to be my baby."

Ros couldn't blink back the tears any longer. They

slid down her cheeks. "I'm sorry he did that to you. I'm sorry I didn't know."

Her mom just wrapped her arms around Ros and held her close. "I'm sorry, too."

Neither one of them noticed Carter disappearing back into the house. Or the whine of the power saw that started all over again.

The knock on her kitchen door that evening was less a surprise than the sight of the two men standing outside. After the events of that morning, Ros wasn't sure how much more she could take.

She looked from Trace to Seamus and back again. "Where's Drake?"

"With his mom." Trace elbowed Seamus. "Well?"

The older man flushed and stuck out a folded sheaf of papers. "I wrote up the list of everybody I could think of who used Poocheez."

She took the pages. "Thank you."

"And uh," Seamus tugged on his ear, "if you need help with your grand opening, I'll be glad to come around."

"And," Trace prompted.

"And I'll reimburse you for whatever repairs you needed to make this place livable." He shot Trace a look. "Within reason, of course."

"Of course," she repeated. It was plain that Seamus was only there because Trace had somehow coerced him into it. "But I understood your finances were tied up elsewhere."

His flush deepened. "I'll be working on getting out of that deal."

"You know, the party responsible for Sherry's expenses is the party responsible for the accident that caused her injuries. What's the trucking company doing about it?"

"Some guy from the insurance company said they would cover the hospital but nothing after that."

"Some *guy*?" She sighed faintly. "Get me his contact information and I'll see what I can do."

Seamus goggled at her. "Why would you do that?"

"Because it's the right thing to do." Looking at Trace made her ache inside and she stepped back to push the door closed.

Trace's hand caught it, though. "Are you okay?"

She was anything but. She wanted to tell him about her mother. She wanted him to hold her in his arms and make the world disappear. "Do you want to stay here with me?"

"Are *you* going to stay here?"

She couldn't answer.

And he knew it. She could see it in his eyes. "G'night, Ros."

She watched him and Seamus walk away.

At least Trace hadn't said goodbye.

Chapter Seventeen

The last Saturday of the month dawned clear and bright. Poocheez was spit-shined and ready. She had an arch of balloons, courtesy of Nell and Archer, swaying gently in front of the building, and bluegrass playing on the speakers that Grant and Ryder had rigged.

Ros was still a nervous wreck.

Even when Drake showed up early, looking heartbreakingly grownup with a fresh haircut, a button-down shirt and cargo shorts that were obviously new because he wasn't already outgrowing them, she could hardly sit still. She paced around, straightening this and adjusting that.

Meanwhile, Drake contentedly munched through several of the cookies her mother had delivered the evening before and swung his leg unconcernedly. "They'll come," he said.

"How's your mom doing?" *How's your dad?* she wanted to ask. She hadn't seen Trace since he and Seamus had shown up on her doorstep the weekend before. Though while she'd been in Braden picking out awning cover fabric with her mom, he'd come by to replace the doorjamb. Almost as if he'd known exactly when to avoid seeing her.

"She's got a physical therapist coming to our house now," Drake said, "so she's getting better moving around with her walker."

Ros didn't ask who was paying for the therapist. It had only taken two phone calls on Sherry's behalf to make sure a more equitable settlement would be forthcoming from the trucking company.

"Did you pick up some flowers to give Sammy Lee for her party later today?" Trace would be picking him up to take him straight from Poocheez to the birthday party.

Drake rolled his eyes. "Yes, my dad's bringing 'em when he gets me, but she's gonna think they're dumb."

"Not forever," Ros promised. The nervous tension was swelling in her stomach. "I'm going out back for a minute. Yell if you need me." She went to the kitchen and filled a glass with water, still marveling that her cupboards were now stocked with actual dishes and glassware, and carried it out the back door where she perched on the edge of one of the chairs Trace had given her.

If she didn't get any business that day, should she take it as a final sign from Poocheez? Or did it mean she just needed to buckle down and work harder to make it a success? And what if she did get a trickle of business? Would it be enough?

She closed her eyes. *Sometimes the only way forward...*

Try as she might, she couldn't stop Trace's words from circling in her head.

If she didn't have doubts herself, wouldn't she have been able to convince him that she was exactly where she wanted to be?

"They're coming."

She jerked up her head. Drake stood in the kitchen doorway, grinning.

"Who?"

He shrugged. "Come 'n see."

She followed him to the front of the building.

Three cars were driving up No Name Road and she didn't recognize a single one.

They were soon followed by nearly a dozen more.

By noon, Drake—manning the appointment book at the front desk—had filled several slots in the coming days and weeks with appointments while Ros stayed busy with the canine clients and Seamus schmoozed with their humans as if he'd been the one to bring them in through the door. She didn't care. She had customers, and for once, she was too busy to think about anything except the tasks at hand.

Several members of her family stopped by. She had to give a little pep talk to Drake when it was time for him to leave for the party because he suddenly thought staying to help her was a better idea. But otherwise, the afternoon passed as quickly as the morning and when Seamus came back to the washing station where she was soothing a trembling miniature poodle, she barely even glanced up.

"There's a woman asking to speak to you. Sounds important."

"I'm a little busy here, Seamus," she pointed out.

He looked resigned. "I can finish washing Misty for you."

So far, he hadn't helped with any particular grooming task, though she had no complaints since he'd been dealing more than adequately with the people. "Sure you remember how?"

He flushed as he took over the task. "I remember. She's outside. Tall and toothy with no dog."

She made her way through the busy waiting area and slipped through the doorway.

The woman was immediately obvious, standing in the shade of the tree and Ros sighed. She recognized a reporter when she saw one. She lifted her chin and approached her. "Good afternoon. Welcome to Poocheez."

"Shonda Simpson. KGWA News." The woman looked past Ros toward the building. "Now I see why you've been so difficult to reach."

"If you're here to ask questions about my father, I have no comment."

"I want to do a story about *you*, Ms. Pastore."

"Unless it's to promote Poocheez, I can't imagine why anyone would be interested."

"Don't underestimate the appeal of human interest. You had a stellar legal career sidelined by your father's scandal. Now you're in line for a judgeship yet here you are in the back of nowhere drumming up doggie business. Everyone loves a comeback story, and you seem primed for it."

Ros gestured at the people milling around them. On her flyer she'd specified the hours as 10:00 to 5:00 and there was no way she'd have everyone finished by then. "I have clients waiting, so I'll wish you a safe drive home. Have a cookie before you go." She turned and froze at the sight of Trace climbing out of his truck, something bundled in one arm.

Everything inside her went soft and suddenly putting one foot in front of the other seemed a monumental effort. Especially when he drew near enough for her to see the white-and-brown spots of the bundle he carried. It was a beagle puppy.

"What d'you think?" He held up the little wriggling pup.

Her stomach tightened. "That's not…not for me, is it?"

"Don't look so panicked. It's for Drake. Figure it's time we got another dog."

She was relieved. At least she told herself she was relieved. "She's darling." She rubbed the dog's silky head.

"Here's my card," Shonda boldly interrupted them. "In case you change your mind."

Ros took the card and shoved it in the pocket of her smock just to get the reporter to move along.

"What's that about?" Trace asked as the woman headed toward the cars parked along the edge of the road.

"Nothing important. Are you getting Drake soon from the party?"

"On my way there now. The vet in Weaver dropped the puppy off just as I was heading out. Was thinking maybe you'd be finishing up here by now." He scanned the people there. "Guess you're still keeping Seamus busy."

"I can manage if he needs to go back to stay with Sherry."

"The physical therapist is still there."

"You could leave the puppy with me and bring Drake here." She practically held her breath as he seemed to consider it. "I could fix dinner, too," she added, cringing at the hint of desperation she heard in her own voice. "My mother gave me a ton of leftovers yesterday." She forced some humor into her tone. "I'll never get through them on my own."

He shifted and moved the puppy from one arm to the other. His eyes stared into hers. "I don't think it'd be a good idea."

Her chest squeezed. "Trace—"

"Congratulations on the turnout here, though." His voice sounded gruff and he suddenly leaned down to brush a kiss across lips. "You've done a helluva job."

Then he turned and strode back to his truck.

A helluva job. But not one that was good enough to convince him she intended to stay.

Two days later, Ros made the four-hour drive to the state penitentiary in Rawlins. When Ros had told Nell of her plans, she'd insisted on going with her.

Whether she wanted to admit it or not, Ros had been relieved. Just because she was taking to heart Trace's words about facing the past before going forward didn't mean she felt all that brave in the process.

They arrived close to noon.

"Are you sure you're ready for this?" Nell was sitting in the passenger seat. They'd found a patch of shade to park in and Nell was nursing Julia, who'd been an angel in her car seat the entire drive.

"Yes." Ros flipped down her visor and checked her appearance. "It's not my first time here at the pen."

"It's your first time visiting your father in one."

She flipped the visor back up. "Do you know that I really *do* like classical music?"

"Ah...okay."

"And I like Motown. The Temptations in particular. And Taylor Swift. And a dozen others but classical most of all."

"It's okay to like classical music, Ros."

"My father listened *only* to classical music."

"So do a couple bazillion other people. Doesn't mean you're just like him."

"Right." She was dithering. And she hated dithering. "Right." She got out of the car and straightened her jacket. She was wearing her favorite black suit. She had her power ponytail. Her Louboutins. "How do I look?"

"Scarily perfect."

"Good," she said, and grabbed her slender briefcase. "Sometimes it's good to be a little scary. After I'm done in there, we're checking into the hotel and I might need an entire jar of peanut butter. And wine."

"I brought provisions."

"That's one of the things I love about you." She closed the door softly so as not to disturb Julia.

Then she crossed the huge parking lot, her high heels clicking with a comfortable, familiar sound.

Even though she'd made advance arrangements, it still took a while to get through the security protocols.

But finally she was sitting there. And so was he.

Martin Pastore. The man who'd been larger-than-life for nearly her whole life.

Even though there had been a part of her that had been afraid of this very moment, of whether or not she'd feel like curling up and disappearing altogether, she realized she wasn't the one who was small. Ineffectual. Harmless.

Her father, in his prison orange uniform, on the other hand, was.

Ros folded her hands in her lap. "Are you being treated well?"

"As well as I can expect." His eyes were dark. Expressionless. "Why are you here?"

"Because I wanted to look you in the face, knowing who you really are."

His lips thinned. He didn't reply. And suddenly, anger blossomed inside her.

"What you did to my mother was despicable."

He sat forward a few inches at that. "*I* made you who you are. Not your mother."

"You may have tutored me to pass the bar. You might have even inspired me to love the law. But you did *not* make me who I am. I don't use people to my own end. I don't dangle my affection at the end of a string like a carrot. I don't accept bribes and blame it on people who trust me. And I am not going to die old and alone the way you will."

"Bravo. You have a mind of your own. *I* taught you that, too."

"Maybe you did, Dad. I don't know if it even matters because the end result is that I do. And I certainly know right from wrong. I don't know if you forgot that somewhere along the way or if you never really knew it at all."

"I gave you everything you ever needed. Wanted. The best education. The best home."

"You gave me a roof over my head," she scoffed. "A beautiful roof. I'll give you that. But still only a roof. It was never a home. And maybe that's why it's taken me this long to recognize it when, by some *miracle*, it lands almost right in my lap."

She stood and caught the guard's eye where he was standing with his back against the wall. "I'm finished here," she told him.

He nodded and started toward them.

She looked back at her father.

"Enjoy your new roof," she said quietly.

Then she turned on her high heel and followed

the guard out of room. Out of the block. Out of the building.

She crossed the parking lot and opened her car door and tossed her briefcase inside.

"Well?" Nell looked worried. "You weren't in there very long at all."

"Long enough," Ros said. Exhilaration replaced anger. "D'you care if we *don't* spend the night at the hotel like we planned?"

Nell's eyebrows rose. "No. I always sleep better when Archer's beside me."

She shuddered just a little because some habits were *really* ingrained. "Then strap my goddaughter back into her car seat. And let's go home."

They made it back to Braden by five.

Ros dropped off Nell and Julia at their place and drove straight to the Bar-H. She knew she was taking a chance that she wouldn't even find Trace there.

He could be out riding fence.

Or fishing with Drake.

Or arguing with Seamus or helping his ex-wife navigate around on her new walker.

Anything was possible.

She just knew that the Bar-H was where she needed to go.

So she did.

His big dusty truck was parked in the drive and she could hear loud music coming from the barn. A cacophony of pounding drums and screaming guitars.

She parked and started walking.

"Ros!" Drake spotted her from where he was sitting on the porch playing with the little beagle puppy.

She didn't break stride. "I need to see your dad first, Drake. Give us a few minutes, okay?"

Trace must have heard because he appeared in the yawning entrance of the barn.

His shirt was blue. His jeans were black. And even from far away, his beard looked very, very dark.

It was all she could do not to break into a run.

He thumbed back his cowboy hat and studied her as she drew nearer. "Is this the look for the new first judicial circuit court judge?" He had to raise his voice above the music.

So did she. "What do you think?" She spread her arms and slowly turned in a circle.

"I think you're perfect."

She smiled slightly and continued walking toward him. She pulled her ponytail free. After another several steps, she kicked off her shoes. Yeah, the gravel was sharp under her feet, but what was a little pain when there was a point to be made?

She shrugged out of her tailored black jacket and tossed it to the ground. Then she took a few more paces and tugged the hem of her red silk camisole from the waist of her pencil skirt.

She stopped two feet in front of him.

Shivers danced down her spine because of the look in his eyes.

"And now? What do you think?"

"I think you're still perfect."

She smiled slightly. "I'm not. I'm a woman first. Lawyer and dog groomer second. And hopefully a friend to anyone who needs it. I'm opinionated. The only things I know how to cook from scratch are scrambled eggs and pancakes. But I can learn. And I will not be the next appointee to the first judicial circuit."

His eyes narrowed. "Ros—"

"I told Judge Potts to keep my name off the list. This time around. Maybe next time I'll consider it." She continued forward again and didn't stop until her bare toes met his dusty cowboy boots. Until she could inhale the scent that was uniquely him. Sagebrush and leather and warmth.

So much warmth it reached all the way through her soul.

She moistened her lips, because as confident as she could act, she was still a trembling mess deep down inside where it mattered the most. "If the position is closer to here," she added.

"To Braden, you mean."

She slid her hands up his chest and felt the hard, heavy heartbeat along the way. "To *you*."

He touched her waist. Lightly. Warily. "Are you going to stay? What about your career?"

"There are four lawyers between me and my brother and sisters," she said. "I'm pretty sure I can keep my hand in law for however long and however deeply I want. As for Poocheez, we'll just have to see how it goes. The grand opening gives me hope. And there's a simple solution for hiring Drake. If he still figures he wants to spend some of his time up to his ears in wet dog hair, that is."

"What's that?"

Her pulse was throbbing inside her head. "His dad just has to marry me. Then we keep it all in the family."

His hands looped behind her back. She could feel the press of his thumbs against her spine. "Thought that kind of thing wasn't your style."

"It wasn't," she whispered. "Until you."

"Did you just propose to me?"

She laughed nervously. "Quite possibly. Are you going to accept?"

The lines beside his eyes crinkled a little. "Most likely."

She sucked in an unsteady breath. "You know Drake's over there watching all this."

"Yep."

"So whatever you're going to do, keep it G-rated. He's impressionable."

"You're the one leaving a trail of clothes behind you," he reminded. His eyes searched hers. "You're sure?"

"Never more." She stretched up on her toes until she could nearly brush his lips with hers. "I love you, gunny," she whispered. "So kiss me. And then I'll know I'm really home."

His smile was slow. His teeth very white. "I love you, too."

Then he lowered his head. Brushed his mouth gently, sweetly, exquisitely, against hers.

And she was home.

* * * * *

If you loved Trace and Ros,
don't miss the next installment of
Return to the Double-C Ranch
by New York Times *bestselling author*
Allison Leigh.

Coming in February 2022 from
Harlequin Special Edition.

Nothing will change how much Colt Dawson loves his baby boy. Not even the shocking news his deceased wife lied about Ryder's paternity. But confronting Ava Guthrie about his ex's sperm-donor scheme doesn't go as planned. Will Ava heal Colt's betrayed heart in time for a Wyoming family Christmas?

Read on for a sneak peek at
His Baby No Matter What,
the next book in the Dawson Family Ranch miniseries by Melissa Senate!

"I wasn't planning on getting one," Ava said. "I figured it would be make me feel sad, celebrating all alone out at the ranch. My parents gone too young. And this year, my great-aunt gone before I even knew her. My best friend after the worst argument I've ever had. I love Christmas, but this is a weird one."

"Yeah, it is. And you're not alone. I'm here. Ryder's here. And like you said, you love Christmas. That house needs some serious cheering up. I want to get you a tree as a gift from me to you for our good deal."

"It *is* a good deal," she said. "Okay. A tree. I have a box of ornaments that I brought over in the move to the ranch."

HSEEXP1021

He pulled out his phone, did some googling and found a Christmas-tree farm that also sold wreaths just ten minutes from here. He held up the site. "Let's go after Ryder's nap. While he's asleep, we can have that meeting—I mean, *talk*—about our arrangement. Set the agenda. The… What would you call it in noncorporate speak?"

She laughed. "Maybe it is a little nice having a CEO around here," she said, then took a bite of her sandwich. "You get things done, Colt Dawson."

He reached over and touched her hand and she squeezed it. Again he was struck by how close he felt to her. But he had to remember he was leaving in two and a half weeks, going back to Bear Ridge, back to his life. There was a 5 percent chance, probably less, that he'd ever leave Godfrey and Dawson. But he'd have this break, this Christmas with his son, on this alpaca ranch.

With a woman who made him think of reaching for the stars, even if he wouldn't.

SPECIAL EXCERPT FROM

Ranch manager Annie McCade thought her twin niece and nephew could join her at the Angel View Ranch for Christmas, with her absent employer being none the wiser. But when the ranch's owner, Tate Sheridan, shows up out of the blue, Annie's plans are upended. Soon she finds herself helping Tate make a Christmas to remember for his grieving and fractured extended family.

Read on for a preview of
New York Times *bestselling author RaeAnne Thayne's heartwarming Christmas romance*
Sleigh Bells Ring*!*

"The tree looks great. Let me take a look at the photograph to see if we're missing anything."

She crossed to Wallace's desk, where they had laid the images out in a row for reference. "There are pine boughs above the mantel. If I remember right, those were real, which helped make it smell like Christmas in here. Maybe when we cut down the tree for the great room, we could save some extra branches to use as greenery on the mantel."

"Good idea," he said gruffly.

This would be a very long day if he didn't figure out a way to put the lid on his growing attraction to her.

He helped Annelise set out various-sized candlesticks on the mantel as well as an exquisite sculpture of an angel with its wings spread wide. Tate guessed the angel was an actual art piece his grandfather had purchased somewhere and then casually stored with the other Angel's View holiday decorations.

"Looks great," he said when they had matched the images from the previous year to the best of their ability.

"It does," Annelise agreed. "That wasn't so bad, was it?"

"I suppose not."

He had to admit, it wasn't the worst morning he had ever spent, talking to a lovely woman who smelled delicious, in a room lit by a cozy fire.

She was completely out-of-bounds, he reminded himself firmly.

"We should probably move on to the next room," she said.

"Right."

He would be better taking that cold walk next to the river. Maybe then he could work out of his system this attraction for someone he shouldn't want.

Don't miss
Sleigh Bells Ring *by RaeAnne Thayne,*
available wherever HQN books and ebooks are sold!